3/06 SET

JAN 03

DATE DUE

THE BIG FOUR

THE BIG FOUR

AGATHA CHRISTIE

BANTAM BOOKS
TORONTO · NEW YORK · LONDON · SYDNEY · AUCKLAND

THE BIG FOUR
*A Bantam Book / published by arrangement with
Dodd, Mead & Company*

Agatha Christie Hardcover Collection / February 1986

*If you would be interested in receiving bookends for The Agatha
Christie Mystery Collection, please write to this address for
information:*

The Agatha Christie Mystery Collection
Bantam Books
P.O. Box 957
Hicksville, N.Y. 11802

ISBN 0-553-35041-2

Published simultaneously in the United States and Canada

PRINTED IN THE UNITED STATES OF AMERICA

0 9 8 7 6 5 4 3 2 1

CONTENTS

THE BIG FOUR

CHAPTER I

THE UNEXPECTED GUEST

I have met people who enjoy a channel crossing; men who can sit calmly in their deck-chairs and, on arrival, wait until the boat is moored, then gather their belongings together without fuss and disembark. Personally, I can never manage this. From the moment I get on board I feel that the time is too short to settle down to anything. I move my suitcases from one spot to another, and if I go down to the saloon for a meal, I bolt my food with an uneasy feeling that the boat may arrive unexpectedly whilst I am below. Perhaps all this is merely a legacy from one's short leaves in the war, when it seemed a matter of such importance to secure a place near the gangway, and to be amongst the first to disembark lest one should waste precious minutes of one's three or five days' leave.

On this particular July morning, as I stood by the rail and watched the white cliffs of Dover drawing nearer, I marvelled at the passengers who could sit calmly in their chairs and never even raise their eyes for the first sight of the native land. Yet perhaps their case was different from mine. Doubtless many of them had only crossed to Paris for the week-end, whereas I had spent the last year and a half on a ranch in the Argentine. I had prospered there, and my wife and I had both enjoyed the free and easy life of the South American continent, nevertheless it was with

1

a lump in my throat that I watched the familiar shore draw nearer and nearer.

I had landed in France two days before, transacted some necessary business, and was now *en route* for London. I should be there some months—time enough to look up old friends, and one old friend in particular. A little man with an egg-shaped head and green eyes—Hercule Poirot! I proposed to take him completely by surprise. My last letter from the Argentine had given no hint of my intended voyage—indeed, that had been decided upon hurriedly as a result of certain business complications—and I spent many amused moments picturing to myself his delight and stupefaction on beholding me.

He, I knew, was not likely to be far from his headquarters. The time when his cases had drawn him from one end of England to the other was past. His fame had spread, and no longer would he allow one case to absorb all his time. He aimed more and more, as time went on, at being considered a "consulting detective"—as much a specialist as a Harley Street physician. He had always scoffed at the popular idea of the human bloodhound who assumed wonderful disguises to track criminals, and who paused at every footprint to measure it.

"No, my friend Hastings," he would say; "we leave that to Giraud and his friends. Hercule Poirot's methods are his own. Order and method, and 'the little gray cells.' Sitting at ease in our own arm-chairs we see the things that these others overlook, and we do not jump to the conclusion like the worthy Japp."

No; there was little fear of finding Hercule Poirot far afield.

On arrival in London, I deposited my luggage at an hotel and drove straight on to the old address. What poignant memories it brought back to me! I hardly waited to greet my old landlady, but hurried up the stairs two at a time and rapped on Poirot's door.

"Enter, then," cried a familiar voice from within.

I strode in. Poirot stood facing me. In his arms he carried a small valise, which he dropped with a crash on beholding me.

"*Mon ami,* Hastings!" he cried. "*Mon ami,* Hastings!"

And, rushing forward, he enveloped me in a capacious embrace. Our conversation was incoherent and inconsequent. Ejaculations, eager questions, incomplete answers, messages from my wife, explanations as to my journey, were all jumbled up together.

"I suppose there's some one in my old rooms?" I asked at last, when we had calmed down somewhat. "I'd love to put up here again with you."

Poirot's face changed with startling suddenness.

"*Mon Dieu!* but what a *chance épouvantable.* Regard around you, my friend."

For the first time I took note of my surroundings. Against the wall stood a vast ark of a trunk of prehistoric design. Near to it were placed a number of suitcases, ranged neatly in order of size from large to small. The inference was unmistakable.

"You are going away?"

"Yes."

"Where to?"

"South America."

"*What?*"

"Yes, it is a droll farce, is it not? It is to Rio I go, and every day I say to myself, I will write nothing in my letters—but oh! the surprise of the good Hastings when he beholds me!"

"But when are you going?"

Poirot looked at his watch.

"In an hour's time."

"I thought you always said nothing would induce you to make a long sea voyage?"

Poirot closed his eyes and shuddered.

"Speak not of it to me, my friend. My doctor, he

assures me that one dies not of it—and it is for the one time only; you understand, that never—never shall I return."

He pushed me into a chair.

"Come, I will tell you how it all came about. Do you know who is the richest man in the world? Richer even than Rockefeller? Abe Ryland."

"The American Soap King?"

"Precisely. One of his secretaries approached me. There is some very considerable, as you would call it, hocus-pocus going on in connection with a big company in Rio. He wished me to investigate matters on the spot. I refused. I told him that if the facts were laid before me, I would give him my expert opinion. But that he professed himself unable to do. I was to be put in possession of the facts only on my arrival out there. Normally, that would have closed the matter. To dictate to Hercule Poirot is sheer impertinence. But the sum offered was so stupendous that for the first time in my life I was tempted by mere money. It was a competence—a fortune! And there was a second attraction—*you*, my friend. For this last year and a half I have been a very lonely old man. I thought to myself, Why not? I am beginning to weary of this unending solving of foolish problems. I have achieved sufficient fame. Let me take this money and settle down somewhere near my old friend."

I was quite affected by this token of Poirot's regard.

"So I accepted," he continued, "and in an hour's time I must leave to catch the boat train. One of life's little ironies, is it not? But I will admit to you, Hastings, that had not the money offered been so big, I might have hesitated, for just lately I have begun a little investigation of my own. Tell me, what is commonly meant by the phrase, 'The Big Four'?"

"I suppose it had its origin at the Versailles Conference, and then there's the famous 'Big Four' in the film world, and the term is used by hosts of smaller fry."

"I see," said Poirot thoughtfully. "I have come across the phrase, you understand, under certain circumstances where none of those explanations would apply. It seems to refer to a gang of international criminals or something of that kind; only—"

"Only what?" I asked, as he hesitated.

"Only that I fancy that it is something on a large scale. Just a little idea of mine, nothing more. Ah, but I must complete my packing. The time advances."

"Don't go," I urged. "Cancel your passage and come out on the same boat with me."

Poirot drew himself up and glanced at me reproachfully.

"Ah, it is that you do not understand! I have passed my word, you comprehend—the word of Hercule Poirot. Nothing but a matter of life or death could detain me now."

"And that's not likely to occur," I murmured ruefully. "Unless at the eleventh hour 'the door opens and the unexpected guest comes in.' "

I quoted the old saw with a slight laugh, and then, in the pause that succeeded it, we both started as a sound came from the inner room.

"What's that?" I cried.

"Ma foi!" retorted Poirot. "It sounds very like your 'unexpected guest' in my bedroom."

"But how can any one be in there? There's no door except into this room."

"Your memory is excellent, Hastings. Now for the deductions."

"The window! But it's a burglar, then? He must have had a stiff climb of it—I should say it was almost impossible."

I had risen to my feet and was striding in the direction of the door when the sound of a fumbling at the handle from the other side arrested me.

The door swung slowly open. Framed in the doorway stood a man. He was coated from head to foot with dust and mud; his face was thin and emaciated. He stared at us for a moment, and then swayed and fell. Poirot hurried to his side, then he looked up and spoke to me.

"Brandy—quickly."

I dashed some brandy into a glass and brought it. Poirot managed to administer a little, and together we raised him and carried him to the couch. In a few minutes he opened his eyes and looked round him with an almost vacant stare.

"What is it you want, monsieur?" said Poirot.

The man opened his lips and spoke in a queer mechanical voice.

"M. Hercule Poirot, 14 Farraway Street."

"Yes, yes; I am he."

The man did not seem to understand, and merely repeated in exactly the same tone:—

"M. Hercule Poirot, 14 Farraway Street."

Poirot tried him with several questions. Sometimes the man did not answer at all; sometimes he repeated the same phrase. Poirot made a sign to me to ring up on the telephone.

"Get Dr. Ridgeway to come round."

The doctor was in luckily; and as his house was only just round the corner, few minutes elapsed before he came bustling in.

"What's all this, eh?"

Poirot gave a brief explanation, and the doctor started examining our strange visitor, who seemed quite unconscious of his presence or ours.

"H'm!" said Dr. Ridgeway, when he had finished. "Curious case."

"Brain fever?" I suggested.

The doctor immediately snorted with contempt.

"Brain fever! Brain fever! No such thing as brain fever. An invention of novelists. No; the man's had a shock of some kind. He's come here under the force of a persistent idea—to find M. Hercule Poirot, 14 Farraway Street—

6

and he repeats those words mechanically without in the least knowing what they mean."

"Aphasia?" I said eagerly.

This suggestion did not cause the doctor to snort quite as violently as my last one had done. He made no answer, but handed the man a sheet of paper and a pencil.

"Let's see what he'll do with that," he remarked.

The man did nothing with it for some moments, then he suddenly began to write feverishly. With equal suddenness he stopped and let both paper and pencil fall to the ground. The doctor picked it up, and shook his head.

"Nothing here. Only the figure 4 scrawled a dozen times, each one bigger than the last. Wants to write 14 Farraway Street, I expect. It's an interesting case—very interesting. Can you possibly keep him here until this afternoon? I'm due at the hospital now, but I'll come back this afternoon and make all arrangements about him. It's too interesting a case to be lost sight of."

I explained Poirot's departure and the fact that I proposed to accompany him to Southampton.

"That's all right. Leave the man here. He won't get into mischief. He's suffering from complete exhaustion. Will probably sleep for eight hours on end. I'll have a word with that excellent Mrs. Funnyface of yours, and tell her to keep an eye on him."

And Dr. Ridgeway bustled out with his usual celerity. Poirot hastily completed his packing, with one eye on the clock.

"The time, it marches with a rapidity unbelievable. Come now, Hastings, you cannot say that I have left you with nothing to do. A most sensational problem. The man from the unknown. Who is he? What is he? Ah, *sapristi*, but I would give two years of my life to have this boat go to-morrow instead of to-day. There is something here very curious—very interesting. But one must have time—*time*. It may be days—or even months—before he will be able to tell us what he came to tell."

"I'll do my best, Poirot," I assured him. "I'll try to be an efficient substitute."

"Ye-es."

His rejoinder struck me as being a shade doubtful. I picked up the sheet of paper.

"If I were writing a story," I said lightly, "I should weave this in with your latest idiosyncrasy and call it *The Mystery of the Big Four.*" I tapped the pencilled figures as I spoke.

And then I started, for our invalid, roused suddenly from his stupor, sat up in his chair and said clearly and distinctly:

"Li Chang Yen."

He had the look of a man suddenly awakened from sleep. Poirot made a sign to me not to speak. The man went on. He spoke in a clear, high voice, and something in his enunciation made me feel that he was quoting from some written report or lecture.

"Li Chang Yen may be regarded as representing the brains of the Big Four. He is the controlling and motive force. I have designated him, therefore, as Number One. Number Two is seldom mentioned by name. He is represented by an 'S' with two lines through it—the sign for a dollar; also by two stripes and a star. It may be conjectured, therefore, that he is an American subject, and that he represents the power of wealth. There seems no doubt that Number Three is a woman, and her nationality French. It is possible that she may be one of the sirens of the *demi-monde,* but nothing is known definitely. Number Four—"

His voice faltered and broke. Poirot leant forward.

"Yes," he prompted eagerly. "Number Four?"

His eyes were fastened on the man's face. Some overmastering terror seemed to be gaining the day; the features were distorted and twisted.

"The destroyer," gasped the man. Then, with a final convulsive movement, he fell back in a dead faint.

"Mon Dieu!" whispered Poirot, "I was right then. I was right."

"You think—?"

He interrupted me.

"Carry him on to the bed in my room. I have not a minute to lose if I would catch my train. Not that I want to catch it. Oh, that I could miss it with a clear conscience! But I gave my word. Come, Hastings!"

Leaving our mysterious visitor in the charge of Mrs. Pearson, we drove away, and duly caught the train by the skin of our teeth. Poirot was alternately silent and loquacious. He would sit staring out of the window like a man lost in a dream, apparently not hearing a word that I said to him. Then, reverting to animation suddenly, he would shower injunctions and commands upon me, and urge the necessity of constant marconigrams.

We had a long fit of silence just after we passed Woking. The train, of course, did not stop anywhere until Southampton; but just here it happened to be held up by a signal.

"Ah! *Sacré mille tonnerres!*" cried Poirot suddenly. "But I have been an imbecile. I see clearly at last. It is undoubtedly the blessed saints who stopped the train. Jump, Hastings, but jump, I tell you."

In an instant he had unfastened the carriage door, and jumped out on the line.

"Throw out the suit-cases and jump yourself."

I obeyed him. Just in time. As I alighted beside him, the train moved on.

"And now, Poirot," I said, in some exasperation, "perhaps you will tell me what all this is about."

"It is, my friend, that I have seen the light."

"That," I said, "is very illuminating to me."

"It should be," said Poirot, "but I fear—I very much fear that it is not. If you can carry two of these valises, I think I can manage the rest."

CHAPTER II

THE MAN FROM THE ASYLUM

FORTUNATELY the train had stopped near a station. A short walk brought us to a garage where we were able to obtain a car, and half an hour later we were spinning rapidly back to London. Then, and not till then, did Poirot deign to satisfy my curiosity.

"You do not see? No more did I. But I see now. Hastings, *I was being got out of the way.*"

"What!"

"Yes. Very cleverly. Both the place and the method were chosen with great knowledge and acumen. They were afraid of me."

"Who were?"

"Those four geniuses who have banded themselves together to work outside the law. A Chinaman, an American, a Frenchwoman, and—another. Pray the good God we arrive back in time, Hastings."

"You think there is danger to our visitor?"

"I am sure of it."

Mrs. Pearson greeted us on arrival. Brushing aside her ecstasies of astonishment on beholding Poirot, we asked for information. It was reassuring. No one had called, and our guest had not made any sign.

With a sigh of relief we went up to the rooms. Poirot crossed the outer one and went through to the inner one. Then he called me, his voice strangely agitated.

"Hastings, he's dead."

I came running to join him. The man was lying as we had left him, but he was dead, and had been dead some time. I rushed out for a doctor. Ridgeway, I knew, would not have returned yet. I found one almost immediately, and brought him back with me.

"He's dead right enough, poor chap. Tramp you've been befriending, eh?"

"Something of the kind," said Poirot evasively. "What was the cause of death, doctor?"

"Hard to say. Might have been some kind of fit. There are signs of asphyxiation. No gas laid on, is there?"

"No, electric light—nothing else."

"And both windows wide open, too. Been dead about two hours, I should say. You'll notify the proper people, won't you?"

He took his departure. Poirot did some necessary telephoning. Finally, somewhat to my surprise, he rang up our old friend Inspector Japp, and asked him if he could possibly come round.

No sooner were these proceedings completed than Mrs. Pearson appeared, her eyes as round as saucers.

"There's a man here from 'Anwell—from the 'Sylum. Did you ever? Shall I show him up?"

We signified assent, and a big burly man in uniform was ushered in.

" 'Morning, gentlemen," he said cheerfully. "I've got reason to believe you've got one of my birds here. Escaped last night, he did."

"He *was* here," said Poirot quietly.

"Not got away again, has he?" asked the keeper, with some concern.

"He is dead."

The man looked more relieved than otherwise.

"You don't say so. Well, I dare say it's best for all parties."

"Was he—dangerous?"

11

" 'Omicidal, d'you mean? Oh, no. 'Armless enough. Persecution mania very acute. Full of secret societies from China that had got him shut up. They're all the same."

I shuddered.

"How long had he been shut up?" asked Poirot.

"A matter of two years now."

"I see," said Poirot quietly. "It never occurred to anybody that he might—be sane?"

The keeper permitted himself to laugh.

"If he was sane, what would he be doing in a lunatic asylum? They all *say* they're sane, you know."

Poirot said no more. He took the man in to see the body. The identification came immediately.

"That's him—right enough," said the keeper callously; "funny sort of bloke, ain't he? Well, gentlemen, I had best go off now and make arrangements under the circumstances. We won't trouble you with the corpse much longer. If there's a hinquest, you will have to appear at it, I dare say. Good morning, sir."

With a rather uncouth bow he shambled out of the room.

A few minutes later Japp arrived. The Scotland Yard Inspector was jaunty and dapper as usual.

"Here I am, Moosior Poirot. What can I do for you? Thought you were off to the coral strands of somewhere or other to-day?"

"My good Japp, I want to know if you have ever seen this man before."

He led Japp into the bedroom. The Inspector stared down at the figure on the bed with a puzzled face.

"Let me see now—he seems sort of familiar—and I pride myself on my memory, too. Why, God bless my soul, it's Mayerling!"

"And who is—or was—Mayerling?"

"Secret Service chap—not one of our people. Went to Russia five years ago. Never heard of again. Always thought the Bolshies had done him in."

"It all fits in," said Poirot, when Japp had taken his leave, "except for the fact that he seems to have died a natural death."

He stood looking down on the motionless figure with a dissatisfied frown. A puff of wind set the window-curtains flying out, and he looked up sharply.

"I suppose you opened the windows when you laid him down on the bed, Hastings?"

"No, I didn't," I replied. "As far as I remember, they were shut."

Poirot lifted his head suddenly.

"Shut—and now they are open. What can that mean?"

"Somebody came in that way," I suggested.

"Possibly," agreed Poirot, but he spoke absently and without conviction. After a minute or two he said:

"That is not exactly the point I had in mind, Hastings. If only one window was open it would not intrigue me so much. It is both windows being open that strikes me as curious."

He hurried into the other room.

"The sitting-room window is open, too. That also we left shut. Ah!"

He bent over the dead man, examining the corners of the mouth minutely. Then he looked up suddenly.

"He has been gagged, Hastings. Gagged and then poisoned."

"Good heavens!" I exclaimed, shocked. "I suppose we shall find out all about it from the postmortem."

"We shall find out nothing. He was killed by inhaling strong prussic acid. It was jammed right under his nose. Then the murderer went away again, first opening all the windows. Hydrocyanic acid is exceedingly volatile, but it has a pronounced smell of bitter almonds. With no trace of the smell to guide them, and no suspicion of foul play, death would be put down to some natural cause by the doctors. So this man was in the Secret Service, Hastings. And five years ago he disappeared in Russia."

"The last two years he's been in the Asylum," I said. "But what of the three years before that?"

Poirot shook his head, and then caught my arm. "The clock, Hastings, look at the clock."

I followed his gaze to the mantelpiece. The clock had stopped at four o'clock.

"*Mon ami,* some one has tampered with it. It had still three days to run. It is an eight-day clock, you comprehend?"

"But what should they want to do that for? Some idea of a false scent by making the crime appear to have taken place at four o'clock?"

"No, no; rearrange your ideas, *mon ami.* Exercise your little gray cells. You are Mayerling. You hear something, perhaps—and you know well enough that your doom is sealed. You have just time to leave a sign. *Four* o'clock, Hastings. Number Four, the *destroyer.* Ah! an idea!"

He rushed into the other room and seized the telephone. He asked for Hanwell.

"You are the Asylum, yes? I understand there has been an escape to-day? What is that you say? A little moment, if you please. Will you repeat that? Ah! *parfaitement.*"

He hung up the receiver, and turned to me. "You heard, Hastings? *There has been no escape.*"

"But the man who came—the keeper?" I said.

"I wonder—I very much wonder."

"You mean—?"

"Number Four—the destroyer."

I gazed at Poirot dumbfounded. A minute or two after, on recovering my voice, I said:—

"We shall know him again, anywhere, that's one thing. He was a man of very pronounced personality."

"Was he, *mon ami?* I think not. He was burly and bluff and red-faced, with a thick moustache and a hoarse voice. He will be none of those things by this time, and for the rest, he has nondescript eyes, nondescript ears, and a per-

14

fect set of false teeth. Identification is not such an easy matter as you seem to think. Next time—"

"You think there will be a next time?" I interrupted.

Poirot's face grew very grave.

"It is a duel to the death, *mon ami*. You and I on the one side, the Big Four on the other. They have won the first trick; but they have failed in their plan to get me out of the way, and in the future they have to reckon with Hercule Poirot!"

CHAPTER III

WE HEAR MORE
ABOUT LI CHANG YEN

FOR a day or two after our visit from the fake Asylum attendant I was in some hopes that he might return, and I refused to leave the flat even for a moment. As far as I could see, he had no reason to suspect that we had penetrated his disguise. He might, I thought, return and try to remove the body, but Poirot scoffed at my reasoning.

"Mon ami," he said, "if you wish you may wait in to put salt on the little bird's tail, but for me I do not waste my time so."

"Well then, Poirot," I argued, "why did he run the risk of coming at all? If he intended to return later for the body, I can see some point in his visit. He would at least be removing the evidence against himself; as it is, he does not seem to have gained anything."

Poirot shrugged his most Gallic shrug. "But you do not see with the eyes of Number Four, Hastings," he said. "You talk of evidence, but what evidence have we against him? True, we have a body, but we have no proof even that the man was murdered—prussic acid, when inhaled, leaves no trace. Again, we can find no one who saw any one enter the flat during our absence, and we have found out nothing about the movements of our late friend, Mayerling. . . .

"No, Hastings, Number Four has left no trace, and he knows it. His visit we may call a reconnaissance. Perhaps he wanted to make quite sure that Mayerling was dead, but more likely, I think, he came to see Hercule Poirot, and to have speech with the adversary whom alone he must fear."

Poirot's reasoning appeared to me typically egotistical, but I forbore to argue.

"And what about the inquest?" I asked. "I suppose you will explain things clearly there, and let the police have a full description of Number Four."

"And to what end? Can we produce anything to impress a coroner's jury of your solid Britishers? Is our description of Number Four of any value? No; we shall allow them to call it 'Accidental Death,' and may be, although I have not much hope, our clever murderer will pat himself on the back that he deceived Hercule Poirot in the first round."

Poirot was right as usual. We saw no more of the man from the asylum, and the inquest, at which I gave evidence, but which Poirot did not even attend, aroused no public interest.

As, in view of his intended trip to South America, Poirot had wound up his affairs before my arrival, he had at this time no cases on hand, but although he spent most of his time in the flat I could get little out of him. He remained buried in an arm-chair, and discouraged my attempts at conversation.

And then one morning, about a week after the murder, he asked me if I would care to accompany him on a visit he wished to make. I was pleased, for I felt he was making a mistake in trying to work things out so entirely on his own, and I wished to discuss the case with him. But I found he was not communicative. Even when I asked where we were going, he would not answer.

Poirot loves being mysterious. He will never part with a piece of information until the last possible moment. In this instance, having taken successively a 'bus and two trains, and arrived in the neighbourhood of one of London's most depressing southern suburbs, he consented at last to explain matters.

"We go, Hastings, to see the one man in England who knows most of the underground life of China."

"Indeed! Who is he?"

"A man you have never heard of—a Mr. John Ingles. To all intents and purposes, he is a retired Civil Servant of mediocre intellect, with a house full of Chinese curios with which he bores his friends and acquaintances. Nevertheless, I am assured by those who should know that the only man capable of giving me the information I seek is this same John Ingles."

A few moments more saw us ascending the steps of The Laurels, as Mr. Ingles's residence was called. Personally, I did not notice a laurel bush of any kind, so deduced that it had been named according to the usual obscure nomenclature of the suburbs.

We were admitted by an impassive-faced Chinese servant and ushered into the presence of his master. Mr. Ingles was a squarely-built man, somewhat yellow of countenance, with deep-set eyes that were oddly reflective in character. He rose to greet us, setting aside an open letter which he had held in his hand. He referred to it after his greeting.

"Sit down, won't you? Halsey tells me that you want some information and that I may be useful to you in the matter."

"That is so, monsieur. I ask of you if you have any knowledge of a man named Li Chang Yen?"

"That's rum—very rum indeed. How did you come to hear about the man?"

"You know him, then?"

"I've met him once. And I know something of him—not quite as much as I should like to. But it surprises me that any one else in England should even have heard of him. He's a great man in his way—mandarin class and all that, you know—but that's not the crux of the matter. There's good reason to suppose that he's the man behind it all."

"Behind what?"

"Everything. The world-wide unrest, the labour troubles that beset every nation, and the revolutions that break out in some. There are people, not scaremongers, who know what they are talking about, and they say that there is a force behind the scenes which aims at nothing less than the disintegration of civilisation. In Russia, you know, there were many signs that Lenin and Trotsky were mere puppets whose every action was dictated by another's brain. I have no definite proof that would count with you, but I am quite convinced that this brain was Li Chang Yen's."

"Oh, come," I protested, "isn't that a bit far-fetched? How would a Chinaman cut any ice in Russia?"

Poirot frowned at me irritably.

"For you, Hastings," he said, "everything is far-fetched that comes not from your own imagination; for me, I agree with this gentleman. But continue, I pray, monsieur."

"What exactly he hopes to get out of it all I cannot pretend to say for certain," went on Mr. Ingles; "but I assume his disease is one that has attacked great brains from the time of Akbar and Alexander to Napoleon—a lust for power and personal supremacy. Up to modern times armed force was necessary for conquest, but in this century of unrest a man like Li Chang Yen can use other means. I have evidence that he has unlimited money behind him for bribery and propaganda, and there are signs that he controls some scientific force more powerful than the world has dreamed of."

Poirot was following Mr. Ingles's words with the closest attention.

"And in China?" he asked. "He moves there too?"

The other nodded in emphatic assent.

"There," he said, "although I can produce no proof that would count in a court of law, I speak from my own knowledge. I know personally every man who counts for anything in China to-day, and this I can tell you: the men who loom most largely in the public eye are men of little or no personality. They are marionettes who dance to the wires pulled by a master hand, and that hand is Li Chang Yen's. His is the controlling brain of the East to-day. We don't understand the East—we never shall; but Li Chang Yen is its moving spirit. Not that he comes out into the limelight—oh, not at all; he never moves from his palace in Pekin. But he pulls strings—that's it, pulls strings—and things happen far away."

"And is there no one to oppose him?" asked Poirot.

Mr. Ingles leant forward in his chair.

"Four men have tried in the last four years," he said slowly; "men of character, and honesty, and brain power. Any one of them might in time have interfered with his plans." He paused.

"Well?" I queried.

"Well, they are dead. One wrote an article, and mentioned Li Chang Yen's name in connection with the riots in Pekin, and within two days he was stabbed in the street. His murderer was never caught. The offences of the other two were similar. In a speech or an article, or in conversation, each linked Li Chang Yen's name with rioting or revolution and within a week of his indiscretion each was dead. One was poisoned; one died of cholera, an isolated case—not part of an epidemic; and one was found dead in his bed. The cause of the last death was never determined, but I was told by a doctor who saw the corpse that it was burnt and shrivelled as though a wave of electrical energy of incredible power had passed through it."

"And Li Chang Yen?" inquired Poirot. "Naturally nothing is traced to him, but there are signs, eh?"

Mr. Ingles shrugged.

"Oh, signs—yes, certainly. And once I found a man who would talk, a brilliant young Chinese chemist who was a protégé of Li Chang Yen's. He came to me one day, this chemist, and I could see that he was on the verge of a nervous breakdown. He hinted to me of experiments on which he'd been engaged in Li Chang Yen's palace under the mandarin's direction—experiments on coolies in which the most revolting disregard for human life and suffering had been shown. His nerve had completely broken, and he was in the most pitiable state of terror. I put him to bed in a top room of my own house, intending to question him the next day—and that, of course, was stupid of me."

"How did they get him?" demanded Poirot.

"That I shall never know. I woke that night to find my house in flames, and was lucky to escape with my life. Investigation showed that a fire of amazing intensity had broken out on the top floor, and the remains of my young chemist friend were charred to a cinder."

I could see from the earnestness with which he had been speaking that Mr. Ingles was a man mounted on his hobby horse, and evidently he, too, realised that he had been carried away, for he laughed apologetically.

"But, of course," he said, "I have no proofs, and you, like the others, will merely tell me that I have a bee in my bonnet."

"On the contrary," said Poirot quietly, "we have every reason to believe your story. We ourselves are more than a little interested in Li Chang Yen."

"Very odd your knowing about him. Didn't fancy a soul in England had ever heard of him. I'd rather like to know how you did come to hear of him—if it's not indiscreet."

"Not in the least, monsieur. A man took refuge in my rooms. He was suffering badly from shock, but he managed to tell us enough to interest us in this Li Chang Yen. He described four people—the Big Four—an organisation hitherto undreamed of. Number One is Li Chang Yen, Number Two is an unknown American, Number Three an equally unknown Frenchwoman, Number Four may be called the executive of the organisation—*the destroyer*. My informant died. Tell me, monsieur, is that phrase known to you at all? The Big Four."

"Not in connection with Li Chang Yen. No, I can't say it is. But I've heard it, or read it, just lately—and in some unusual connection too. Ah, I've got it."

He rose and went across to an inlaid lacquer cabinet—an exquisite thing, as even I could see. He returned with a letter in his hand.

"Here you are. Note from an old sea-faring man I ran against once in Shanghai. Hoary old reprobate—maudlin with drink by now, I should say. I took this to be the ravings of alcoholism."

He read it aloud:—

"DEAR SIR,—You may not remember me, but you did me a good turn once in Shanghai. Do me another now. I must have money to get out of the country. I'm well hid here, I hope, but any day they may get me. The Big Four, I mean. It's life or death. I've plenty of money, but I daren't get at it, for fear of putting them wise. Send me a couple of hundred in notes. I'll repay it faithful—I swear to that.—Your servant, sir,

"JONATHAN WHALLEY."

"Dated from Granite Bungalow, Hoppaton, Dartmoor. I'm afraid I regarded it as rather a crude method of relieving me of a couple of hundred which I can ill spare. If it's any use to you—" He held it out.

"*Je vous remercie,* monsieur. I start for Hoppaton *à l'heure même.*"

"Dear me, this is very interesting. Supposing I came along too? Any objection?"

"I should be charmed to have your company, but we must start at once. We shall not reach Dartmoor until close on nightfall, as it is."

John Ingles did not delay us more than a couple of minutes, and soon we were in the train moving out of Paddington bound for the West Country. Hoppaton was a small village clustering in a hollow right on the fringe of the moorland. It was reached by a nine-mile drive from Moretonhamstead. It was about eight o'clock when we arrived; but as the month was July, the daylight was still abundant.

We drove into the narrow street of the village and then stopped to ask our way of an old rustic.

"Granite Bungalow," said the old man reflectively, "it be Granite Bungalow you do want? Eh?"

We assured him that this was what we did want.

The old man pointed to a small gray cottage at the end of the street.

"There be t'Bungalow. Do yee want to see t'Inspector?"

"What Inspector?" asked Poirot sharply; "what do you mean?"

"Haven't yee heard about t'murder, then? A shocking business t'was seemingly. Pools of blood, they do say."

"Mon Dieu!" murmured Poirot. "This Inspector of yours, I must see him at once."

Five minutes later we were closeted with Inspector Meadows. The Inspector was inclined to be stiff at first, but at the magic name of Inspector Japp of Scotland Yard, he unbent.

"Yes, sir; murdered this morning. A shocking business. They 'phoned to Moreton, and I came out at once. Looked a mysterious thing to begin with. The old man—he was about seventy, you know, and fond of his glass, from all I hear—was lying on the floor of the living-room. There was a bruise on his head and his throat was cut from ear to ear. Blood all over the place, as you can understand. The woman who cooks for him, Betsy Andrews, she told us that her master had several little Chinese jade figures, that he'd told her were very valuable, and these had disappeared. That, of course, looked like assault and robbery; but there were all sorts of difficulties in the way of that solution. The old fellow had two people in the house; Betsy Andrews, who is a Hoppaton woman, and a rough kind of man-servant, Robert Grant. Grant had gone to the farm to fetch the milk, which he does every day, and Betsy had stepped out to have a chat with a neighbour. She was only away twenty minutes—between ten and half-past—and the crime must have been done then. Grant returned to the house first. He went in by the back door, which was open—no one locks up doors round here—not in broad daylight, at all events—put the milk in the larder, and went into his own room to read the paper and have a smoke. Had no idea anything unusual had occurred—at least, that's what he says. Then Betsy comes in, goes into the living-room, sees what's happened, and lets out a screech to wake the dead. That's all fair and square. Some one got in whilst those two were out, and did the poor old man in. But it struck me at once that he must be a pretty cool customer. He'd have to come right up the village street, or creep through some one's back yard. Granite Bungalow has got houses all round it, as you can see. How was it that no one had seen him?"

The Inspector paused with a flourish.

"Aha, I perceive your point," said Poirot. "To continue?"

"Well, sir, fishy, I said to myself—fishy. And I began to look about me. Those jade figures, now. Would a common tramp ever suspect that they were valuable? Anyway, it was madness to try such a thing in broad daylight. Suppose the old man had yelled for help?"

"I suppose, Inspector," said Mr. Ingles, "that the bruise on the head was inflicted before death?"

"Quite right, sir. First knocked him silly, the murderer did, and then cut his throat. That's clear enough. But how the dickens did he come or go? They notice strangers quick enough in a little place like this. It came to me all at once—nobody did come. I took a good look round. It had rained the night before, and there were footprints clear enough going in and out of the kitchen. In the living-room there were two sets of footprints only (Betsy Andrews's

stopped at the door)—Mr. Whalley's (he was wearing carpet slippers) and another man's. The other man had stepped
in the blood-stains, and I traced his bloody footprints—I
beg your pardon, sir."

"Not at all," said Mr. Ingles, with a faint smile; "the
adjective is perfectly understood."

"I traced them to the kitchen—but not beyond. Point
Number One. On the lintel of Robert Grant's door was a
faint smear—a smear of blood. That's point Number Two.
Point Number Three was when I got hold of Grant's boots—
which he had taken off—and fitted them to the marks.
That settled it. It was an inside job. I warned Grant and
took him into custody; and what do you think I found
packed away in his portmanteau? The little jade figures
and a ticket-of-leave. Robert Grant was also Abraham Biggs,
convicted for felony and housebreaking five years ago."

The Inspector paused triumphantly.

"What do you think of that, gentlemen?"

"I think," said Poirot, "that it appears a very clear
case—of a surprising clearness, in fact. This Biggs, or Grant,
he must be a man very foolish and uneducated, eh?"

"Oh, he is that—a rough, common sort of fellow. No
idea of what a footprint may mean."

"Clearly he reads not the detective fiction! Well, Inspector, I congratulate you. We may look at the scene of the
crime. Yes?"

"I'll take you there myself this minute. I'd like you to
see those footprints."

"I, too, should like to see them. Yes, yes, very interesting, very ingenious."

We set out forthwith. Mr. Ingles and the Inspector
forged ahead. I drew Poirot back a little so as to be able to
speak to him out of the Inspector's hearing.

"What do you really think, Poirot. Is there more in this
than meets the eye?"

"That is just the question, *mon ami*. Whalley says
plainly enough in his letter that the Big Four are on his

track, and we know, you and I, that the Big Four is no bogey for the children. Yet everything seems to say that this man Grant committed the crime. Why did he do so? For the sake of the little jade figures? Or is he an agent of the Big Four? I confess that this last seems more likely. However valuable the jade, a man of that class was not likely to realise the fact—at any rate, not to the point of committing murder for them. (That, *par exemple*, ought to have struck the Inspector.) He could have stolen the jade and made off with it instead of committing a brutal and quite purposeless murder. Ah, yes; I fear our Devonshire friend has not used his little gray cells. He has measured footprints, and has omitted to reflect and arrange his ideas with the necessary order and method."

CHAPTER IV

THE IMPORTANCE OF A LEG OF MUTTON

THE Inspector drew a key from his pocket and unlocked the door of Granite Bungalow. The day had been fine and dry, so our feet were not likely to leave any prints; nevertheless we wiped them carefully on the mat before entering.

A woman came up out of the gloom and spoke to the Inspector, and he turned aside. Then he spoke over his shoulder.

"Have a good look round, Mr. Poirot, and see all there is to be seen. I'll be back in about ten minutes. By the way, here's Grant's boot. I brought it along with me for you to compare the impressions."

We went into the living-room, and the sound of the Inspector's footsteps died away outside. Ingles was attracted immediately by some Chinese curios on a table in the corner, and went over to examine them. He seemed to take no interest in Poirot's doings. I, on the other hand, watched him with breathless interest. The floor was covered with a dark-green linoleum which was ideal for showing up footprints. A door at the farther end led into the small kitchen. From there another door led into the scullery (where the back door was situated), and another into the bedroom which had been occupied by Robert Grant. Having explored the ground, Poirot commented upon it in a low running monologue.

"Here is where the body lay; that big dark stain and

the splashes all around mark the spot. Traces of carpet slippers and 'number nine' boots, you observe, but all very confused. Then two sets of tracks leading to and from the kitchen; whoever the murderer was, he came in that way. You have the boot, Hastings? Give it to me." He compared it carefully with the prints. "Yes, both made by the same man, Robert Grant. He came in that way, killed the old man, and went back to the kitchen. He had stepped in the blood; see the stains he left as he went out? Nothing to be seen in the kitchen—all the village has been walking about in it. He went into his own room—no, first he went back again to the scene of the crime—was that to get the little jade figures? Or had he forgotten something that might incriminate him?"

"Perhaps he killed the old man the second time he went in?" I suggested.

"*Mais non,* you do not observe. On one of the outgoing footmarks stained with blood there is super-imposed an ingoing one. I wonder what he went back for—the little jade figures as an afterthought? It is all ridiculous—stupid."

"Well, he's given himself away pretty hopelessly."

"*N'est-ce pas?* I tell you, Hastings, it goes against reason. It offends my little gray cells. Let us go into his bedroom—ah, yes; there is the smear of blood on the lintel and just a trace of footmarks—the blood-stained, Robert Grant's footmarks, and his only, near the body—Robert Grant the only man who went near the house. Yes, it must be so."

"What about the old woman?" I said suddenly. "She was in the house alone after Grant had gone for the milk. She might have killed him and then gone out. Her feet would leave no prints if she hadn't been outside."

"Very good, Hastings. I wondered whether that hypothesis would occur to you. I had already thought of it and rejected it. Betsy Andrews is a local woman, well known hereabouts. She can have no connection with the

Big Four; and, besides, old Whalley was a powerful fellow, by all accounts. This is a man's work—not a woman's."

"I suppose the Big Four couldn't have had some diabolical contrivance concealed in the ceiling—something which descended automatically and cut the old man's throat and was afterwards drawn up again?"

"Like Jacob's ladder? I know, Hastings, that you have an imagination of the most fertile—but I implore of you to keep it within bounds."

I subsided, abashed. Poirot continued to wander about, poking into rooms and cupboards with a profoundly dissatisfied expression on his face. Suddenly he uttered an excited yelp, reminiscent of a Pomeranian dog. I rushed to join him. He was standing in the larder in a dramatic attitude. In his hand he was brandishing a leg of mutton!

"My dear Poirot!" I cried. "What is the matter? Have you suddenly gone mad?"

"Regard, I pray you, this mutton. But regard it closely!"

I regarded it as closely as I could, but could see nothing unusual about it. It seemed to me a very ordinary leg of mutton. I said as much. Poirot threw me a withering glance.

"But do you not see this—and this—and this—"

He illustrated each "this" with a jab at the unoffending joint, dislodging small icicles as he did so.

Poirot had just accused me of being imaginative, but I now felt that he was far more wildly so than I had ever been. Did he seriously think these slivers of ice were crystals of a deadly poison? That was the only construction I could put upon his extraordinary agitation.

"It's frozen meat," I explained gently. "Imported, you know. New Zealand."

He stared at me for a moment or two and then broke into a strange laugh.

"How marvellous is my friend Hastings! He knows everything—but everything! How do they say—Inquire Within Upon Everything. That is my friend Hastings."

He flung down the leg of mutton onto its dish again and left the larder. Then he looked through the window.

"Here comes our friend the Inspector. It is well. I have seen all I want to see here." He drummed on the table absent-mindedly, as though absorbed in calculation, and then asked suddenly, "What is the day of the week, *mon ami?*"

"Monday," I said, rather astonished. "What—?"

"Ah! Monday, is it? A bad day of the week. To commit a murder on a Monday is a mistake."

Passing back to the living-room, he tapped the glass on the wall and glanced at the thermometer.

"Set fair, and seventy degrees Fahrenheit. An orthodox English summer's day."

Ingles was still examining various pieces of Chinese pottery.

"You do not take much interest in this inquiry, monsieur?" said Poirot.

The other gave a slow smile.

"It's not my job, you see. I'm a connoisseur of some things, but not of this. So I just stand back and keep out of the way. I've learnt patience in the East."

The Inspector came bustling in, apologising for having been so long away. He insisted on taking us over most of the ground again, but finally we got away.

"I must appreciate your thousand politenesses, Inspector," said Poirot, as we were walking down the village street again. "There is just one more request I should like to put to you."

"You want to see the body, perhaps, sir?"

"Oh, dear me, no! I have not the least interest in the body. I want to see Robert Grant."

"You'll have to drive back with me to Moreton to see him, sir."

"Very well, I will do so. But I must see him and be able to speak to him alone."

The Inspector caressed his upper lip.

"Well, I don't know about that, sir."

"I assure you that if you can get through to Scotland Yard you will receive full authority."

"I've heard of you, of course, sir, and I know you've done us a good turn now and again. But it's very irregular."

"Nevertheless, it is necessary," said Poirot calmly. "It is necessary for this reason—Grant is not the murderer."

"What? Who is, then?"

"The murderer was, I should fancy, a youngish man. He drove up to Granite Bungalow in a trap, which he left outside. He went in, committed the murder, came out, and drove away again. He was bare-headed, and his clothing was slightly blood-stained."

"But—but the whole village would have seen him!"

"Not under certain circumstances."

"Not if it was dark, perhaps; but the crime was committed in broad daylight."

Poirot merely smiled.

"And the horse and trap, sir—how could you tell that? Any amount of wheeled vehicles have passed along outside. There's no mark of one in particular to be seen."

"Not with the eyes of the body, perhaps; but with the eyes of the mind, yes."

The Inspector touched his forehead significantly with a grin at me. I was utterly bewildered, but I had faith in Poirot. Further discussion ended in our all driving back to Moreton with the Inspector. Poirot and I were taken to Grant, but a constable was to be present during the interview. Poirot went straight to the point.

"Grant, I know you to be innocent of this crime. Relate to me in your own words exactly what happened."

The prisoner was a man of medium height, with a somewhat unpleasing cast of features. He looked a jailbird if ever a man did.

"Honest to God, I never did it," he whined. "Some one put those little glass figures amongst my traps. It was a frame-up, that's what it was. I went straight to my rooms

31

when I came in, like I said. I never knew a thing till Betsy screeched out. S'welp me, God, I didn't."

Poirot rose.

"If you can't tell me the truth, that is the end of it."

"But, guv'nor—"

"You *did* go into the room—you *did* know your master was dead; and you were just preparing to make a bolt of it when the good Betsy made her terrible discovery."

The man stared at Poirot with a dropped jaw.

"Come now, is it not so? I tell you solemnly—on my word of honour—that to be frank now is your only chance."

"I'll risk it," said the man suddenly. "It was just as you say. I came in, and went straight to the master—and there he was, dead on the floor and blood all round. Then I got the wind up proper. They'd ferret out my record, and for a certainty they'd say it was me as had done him in. My only thought was to get away—at once—before he was found—"

"And the jade figures?"

The man hesitated.

"You see—"

"You took them by a kind of reversion to instinct, as it were? You had heard your master say that they were valuable, and you felt you might as well go the whole hog. That, I understand. Now, answer me this. Was it the second time that you went into the room that you took the figures?"

"I didn't go in a second time. Once was enough for me."

"You are sure of that?"

"Absolutely certain."

"Good. Now, when did you come out of prison?"

"Two months ago."

"How did you obtain this job?"

"Through one of them Prisoners' Help Societies. Bloke met me when I came out."

"What was he like?"

"Not exactly a parson, but looked like one. Soft black

32

hat and mincing way of talking. Got a broken front tooth. Spectacled chap. Saunders his name was. Said he hoped I was repentant, and that he'd find me a good post. I went to old Whalley on his recommendation."

Poirot rose once more.

"I thank you. I know all now. Have patience." He paused in the doorway and added: "Saunders gave you a pair of boots, didn't he?"

Grant looked very astonished.

"Why, yes, he did. But how did you know?"

"It is my business to know things," said Poirot gravely.

After a word or two to the Inspector, the three of us went to the White Hart and discussed eggs and bacon and Devonshire cider.

"Any elucidations yet?" asked Ingles, with a smile.

"Yes, the case is clear enough now; but, see you, I shall have a good deal of difficulty in proving it. Whalley was killed by order of the Big Four—but not by Grant. A very clever man got Grant the post and deliberately planned to make him the scapegoat—an easy matter with Grant's prison record. He gave him a pair of boots, one of two duplicate pairs. The other he kept himself. It was all so simple. When Grant is out of the house, and Betsy is chatting in the village (which she probably did everyday of her life), he drives up wearing the duplicate boots, enters the kitchen, goes through into the living-room, fells the old man with a blow, and then cuts his throat. Then he returns to the kitchen, removes the boots, puts on another pair, and, carrying the first pair, goes out to his trap and drives off again."

Ingles looked steadily at Poirot.

"There's a catch in it still. Why did nobody see him?"

"Ah! That is where the cleverness of Number Four, I am convinced, comes in. Everybody saw him—and yet nobody saw him. You see, he drove up in a butcher's cart!"

I uttered an exclamation.

"The leg of mutton?"

"Exactly, Hastings, the leg of mutton. Everybody swore that no one had been to Granite Bungalow that morning, but, nevertheless, I found in the larder a leg of mutton, still frozen. It was Monday, so the meat must have been delivered that morning; for if on Saturday, in this hot weather, it would not have remained frozen over Sunday. So some one *had* been to the Bungalow, and a man on whom a trace of blood here and there would attract no attention."

"Damned ingenious!" cried Ingles approvingly.

"Yes, he is clever, Number Four."

"As clever as Hercule Poirot?" I murmured.

My friend threw me a glance of dignified reproach.

"There are some jests that you should not permit yourself, Hastings," he said sententiously. "Have I not saved an innocent man from being sent to the gallows? That is enough for one day."

CHAPTER V

DISAPPEARANCE OF A SCIENTIST

PERSONALLY, I don't think that, even when a jury had acquitted Robert Grant, alias Biggs, of the murder of Jonathan Whalley, Inspector Meadows was entirely convinced of his innocence. The case which he had built up against Grant—the man's record, the jade which he had stolen, the boots which fitted the footprints so exactly—was to his matter-of-fact mind too complete to be easily upset; but Poirot, compelled much against his inclination to give evidence, convinced the jury. Two witnesses were produced who had seen a butcher's cart drive up to the bungalow on that Monday morning, and the local butcher testified that his cart only called there on Wednesdays and Fridays.

A woman was actually found who, when questioned, remembered seeing the butcher's man leaving the bungalow, but she could furnish no useful description of him. The only impression he seemed to have left on her mind was that he was clean-shaven, of medium height, and looked exactly like a butcher's man. At this description Poirot shrugged his shoulders philosophically.

"It is as I tell you, Hastings," he said to me, after the trial. "He is an artist, this one. He disguises himself not with the false beard and the blue spectacles. He alters his features, yes; but that is the least part. For the time being he *is* the man he would be. He lives in his part."

Certainly I was compelled to admit that the man who

had visited us from Hanwell had fitted in exactly with my idea of what an asylum attendant should look like. I should never for a moment have dreamt of doubting that he was genuine.

It was all a little discouraging, and our experience on Dartmoor did not seem to have helped us at all. I said as much to Poirot, but he would not admit that we had gained nothing.

"We progress," he said; "we progress. At every contact with this man we learn a little of his mind and his methods. Of us and our plans he knows nothing."

"And there, Poirot," I protested, "he and I seem to be in the same boat. You don't seem to me to have any plans, you seem to sit and wait for him to do something."

Poirot smiled.

"*Mon ami,* you do not change. Always the same Hastings, who would be up and at their throats. Perhaps," he added, as a knock sounded on the door, "you have here your chance; it may be our friend who enters." And he laughed at my disappointment when Inspector Japp and another man entered the room.

"Good evening, moosior," said the Inspector. "Allow me to introduce Captain Kent of the United States Secret Service."

Captain Kent was a tall, lean American, with a singularly impassive face which looked as though it had been carved out of wood.

"Pleased to meet you, gentlemen," he murmured, as he shook hands jerkily.

Poirot threw an extra log on the fire, and brought forward more easy-chairs. I brought out glasses and the whisky and soda. The captain took a deep draught, and expressed appreciation.

"Legislation in your country is still sound," he observed.

"And now to business," said Japp. "Moosior Poirot here made a certain request to me. He was interested in some concern that went by the name of the Big Four, and he asked me to let him know at any time if I came across a mention of it in my official line of business. I didn't take much stock in the matter, but I remembered what he said, and when the captain here came over with rather a curious story, I said at once, 'We'll go round to Moosior Poirot's.' "

Poirot looked across at Captain Kent, and the American took up the tale.

"You may remember reading, M. Poirot, that a number of torpedo boats and destroyers were sunk by being dashed upon the rocks off the American coast. It was just after the Japanese earthquake, and the explanation given was that the disaster was the result of a tidal wave. Now, a short time ago, a round-up was made of certain crooks and gunmen, and with them were captured some papers which put an entirely new face upon the matter. They appeared to refer to some organisation called the 'Big Four,' and gave an incomplete description of some powerful wireless installation—a concentration of wireless energy far beyond anything so far attempted, and capable of focusing a beam of great intensity upon some given spot. The claims made for this invention seemed manifestly absurd, but I turned them in to headquarters for what they were worth, and one of our highbrow professors got busy on them. Now it appears that one of your British scientists read a paper upon the subject before the British Association. His colleagues didn't think great shakes of it, by all accounts, thought it far-fetched and fanciful, but your scientist stuck to his guns, and declared that he himself was on the eve of success in his experiments."

"*Eh bien?*" demanded Poirot, with interest.

"It was suggested that I should come over here and get an interview with this gentleman. Quite a young fellow, he is, Halliday by name. He is the leading authority on the subject, and I was to get from him whether the thing suggested was anyway possible."

"And was it?" I asked eagerly.

"That's just what I don't know. I haven't seen Mr. Halliday—and I'm not likely to, by all accounts."

"The truth of the matter is," said Japp, shortly, "Halliday's disappeared."

"When?"

"Two months ago."

"Was his disappearance reported?"

"Of course it was. His wife came to us in a great state. We did what we could, but I knew all along it would be no good."

"Why not?"

"Never is—when a man disappears that way." Japp winked.

"What way?"

"Paris."

"So Halliday disappeared in Paris?"

"Yes. Went over there on scientific work—so he said. Of course, he'd have to say something like that. But you know what it means when a man disappears over there. Either it's Apache work, and that's the end of it—or else it's voluntary disappearance—and that's a great deal the commoner of the two, I can tell you. Gay Paree and all that, you know. Sick of home life. Halliday and his wife had had a tiff before he started, which all helps to make it a pretty clear case."

"I wonder," said Poirot thoughtfully.

The American was looking at him curiously.

"Say, mister," he drawled, "what's this Big Four idea?"

"The Big Four," said Poirot, "is an international organisation which has at its head a Chinaman. He is known as Number One. Number Two is an American. Number Three is a Frenchwoman. Number Four, the 'Destroyer,' is an Englishman."

"A Frenchwoman, eh?" The American whistled. "And Halliday disappeared in France. Maybe there's something in this. What's her name?"

"I don't know. I know nothing about her."

38

"But it's a mighty big proposition, eh?" suggested the other.

Poirot nodded, as he arranged the glasses in a neat row on the tray. His love of order was as great as ever.

"What was the idea in sinking those boats? Are the Big Four a German stunt?"

"The Big Four are for themselves—and for themselves only, M. le Capitaine. Their aim is world domination."

The American burst out laughing, but broke off at the sight of Poirot's serious face.

"You laugh, monsieur," said Poirot, shaking a finger at him. "You reflect not—you use not the little gray cells of the brain. Who are these men who send a portion of your navy to destruction simply as a trial of their power? For that was all it was, monsieur, a test of this new force of magnetical attraction which they hold."

"Go on with you, moosior," said Japp good-humouredly. "I've read of super criminals many a time, but I've never come across them. Well, you've heard Captain Kent's story. Anything further I can do for you?"

"Yes, my good friend. You can give me the address of Mrs. Halliday—and also a few words of introduction to her if you will be so kind."

Thus it was that the following day saw us bound for Chetwynd Lodge, near the village of Chobham in Surrey.

Mrs. Halliday received us at once, a tall, fair woman, nervous and eager in manner. With her was her little girl, a beautiful child of five.

Poirot explained the purpose of our visit.

"Oh! Monsieur Poirot, I am so glad, so thankful. I have heard of you, of course. You will not be like these Scotland Yard people, who will not listen or try to understand. And the French Police are just as bad—worse, I think. They are all convinced that my husband has gone off with some other woman. But he wasn't like that! All he thought of in life was his work. Half our quarrels came from that. He cared for it more than he did for me."

"Englishmen, they are like that," said Poirot soothingly. "And if it is not work, it is the games, the sport. All those things they take *au grand sérieux*. Now, madame, recount to me exactly, in detail, and as methodically as you can, the exact circumstances of your husband's disappearance."

"My husband went to Paris on Thursday, the 20th of July. He was to meet and visit various people there connected with his work, amongst them Madame Olivier."

Poirot nodded at the mention of the famous French woman chemist, who had eclipsed even Madame Curie in the brilliance of her achievements. She had been decorated by the French Government, and was one of the most prominent personalities of the day.

"He arrived there in the evening and went at once to the Hotel Castiglione in the Rue de Castiglione. On the following morning, he had an appointment with Professor Bourgoneau, which he kept. His manner was normal and pleasant. The two men had a most interesting conversation, and it was arranged that he should witness some experiments in the professor's laboratory on the following day. He lunched alone at the Café Royal, went for a walk in the Bois, and then visited Madame Olivier at her house at Passy. There, also, his manner was perfectly normal. He left about six. Where he dined is not known, probably alone at some restaurant. He returned to the hotel about eleven o'clock and went straight up to his room, after inquiring if any letters had come for him. On the following morning, he walked out of the hotel, and has not been seen again."

"At what time did he leave the hotel? At the hour when he would normally leave it to keep his appointment at Professor Bourgoneau's laboratory?"

"We do not know. He was not remarked leaving the hotel. But no *petit déjeuner* was served to him, which seems to indicate that he went out early."

"Or he might, in fact, have gone out again after he came in the night before?"

"I do not think so. His bed had been slept in, and the night porter would have remembered any one going out at that hour."

"A very just observation, madame. We may take it, then, that he left early on the following morning—and that is reassuring from one point of view. He is not likely to have fallen a victim to any Apache assault at that hour. His baggage, now, was it all left behind?"

Mrs. Halliday seemed rather reluctant to answer, but at last she said:—

"No—he must have taken one small suitcase with him."

"H'm," said Poirot thoughtfully, "I wonder where he was that evening. If we knew that, we should know a great deal. Whom did he meet?—there lies the mystery. Madame, myself I do not of necessity accept the view of the police; with them it is always 'Cherchez la femme.' Yet it is clear that something occurred that night to alter your husband's plans. You say he asked for letters on returning to the hotel. Did he receive any?"

"One only, and that must have been the one I wrote him on the day he left England."

Poirot remained sunk in thought for a full minute, then he rose briskly to his feet.

"Well, madame, the solution of the mystery lies in Paris, and to find it I myself journey to Paris on the instant."

"It is all a long time ago, monsieur."

"Yes, yes. Nevertheless, it is there that we must seek."

He turned to leave the room, but paused with his hand on the door.

"Tell me, madame, do you ever remember your husband mentioning the phrase, 'The Big Four'?"

"The Big Four," she repeated thoughtfully. "No, I can't say I do."

CHAPTER VI

THE WOMAN
ON THE STAIRS

THAT was all that could be elicited from Mrs. Halliday. We hurried back to London, and the following day saw us *en route* for the Continent. With rather a rueful smile, Poirot observed:—

"This Big Four, they make me to bestir myself, *mon ami*. I run up and down, all over the ground, like our old friend 'the human foxhound.' "

"Perhaps you'll meet him in Paris," I said, knowing that he referred to a certain Giraud, one of the most trusted detectives of the Sureté, whom he had met on a previous occasion.

Poirot made a grimace. "I devoutly hope not. He loved me not, that one."

"Won't it be a very difficult task?" I asked. "To find out what an unknown Englishman did on an evening two months ago?"

"Very difficult, *mon ami*. But, as you know well, difficulties rejoice the heart of Hercule Poirot."

"You think the Big Four kidnapped him?"

Poirot nodded.

Our inquiries necessarily went over old ground, and we learnt little to add to what Mrs. Halliday had already told us. Poirot had a lengthy interview with Professor Bourgoneau, during which he sought to elicit whether

Halliday had mentioned any plan of his own for the evening, but we drew a complete blank.

Our next source of information was the famous Madame Olivier. I was quite excited as we mounted the steps of her villa at Passy. It has always seemed to me extraordinary that a woman should go so far in the scientific world. I should have thought a purely masculine brain was needed for such work.

The door was opened by a young lad of seventeen or thereabouts, who reminded me vaguely of an acolyte, so ritualistic was his manner. Poirot had taken the trouble to arrange our interview beforehand, as he knew Madame Olivier never received any one without an appointment, being immersed in research work most of the day.

We were shown into a small *salon,* and presently the mistress of the house came to us there. Madame Olivier was a very tall woman, her tallness accentuated by the long white overall she wore, and a coif like a nun's that shrouded her head. She had a long pale face, and wonderful dark eyes that burnt with a light almost fanatical. She looked more like a priestess of old than a modern Frenchwoman. One cheek was disfigured by a scar, and I remembered that her husband and co-worker had been killed in an explosion in the laboratory three years before, and that she herself had been terribly burned. Ever since then she had shut herself away from the world, and plunged with fiery energy into the work of scientific research. She received us with cold politeness.

"I have been interviewed by the police many times, messieurs. I think it hardly likely that I can help you, since I have not been able to help them."

"Madame, it is possible that I shall not ask you quite the same questions. To begin with, of what did you talk together, you and M. Halliday?"

She looked a trifle surprised.

"But of his work! His work—and also mine."

"Did he mention to you the theories he had embodied recently in his paper read before the British Association?"

"Certainly he did. It was chiefly of those we spoke."

"His ideas were somewhat fantastic, were they not?" asked Poirot carelessly.

"Some people have thought so. I do not agree."

"You considered them practicable?"

"Perfectly practicable. My own line of research has been somewhat similar, though not undertaken with the same end in view. I have been investigating the *gamma* rays emitted by the substance usually known as Radium C., a product of Radium emanation, and in doing so I have come across some very interesting magnetical phenomena. Indeed, I have a theory as to the actual nature of the force we call magnetism, but it is not yet time for my discoveries to be given to the world. Mr. Halliday's experiments and views were exceedingly interesting to me."

Poirot nodded. Then he asked a question which surprised me.

"Madame, where did you converse on these topics? In here?"

"No, monsieur. In the laboratory."

"May I see it?"

"Certainly."

She led the way to the door from which she had entered. It opened on a small passage. We passed through two doors and found ourselves in the big laboratory, with its array of beakers and crucibles and a hundred appliances of which I did not even know the names. There were two occupants, both busy with some experiment. Madame Olivier introduced them.

"Mademoiselle Claude, one of my assistants." A tall, serious-faced young girl bowed to us. "Monsieur Henri, an old and trusted friend."

The young man, short and dark, bowed jerkily.

Poirot looked round him. There were two other doors besides the one by which we had entered. One, madame explained, led into the garden, the other into a smaller chamber also devoted to research. Poirot took all this in, then declared himself ready to return to the salon.

"Madame, were you alone with M. Halliday during your interview?"

"Yes, monsieur. My two assistants were in the smaller room next door."

"Could your conversation be overheard—by them or any one else?"

Madame reflected, then shook her head.

"I do not think so. I am almost sure it could not. The doors were all shut."

"Could any one have been concealed in the room?"

"There is the big cupboard in the corner—but the idea is absurd."

"*Pas tout à fait,* madame. One thing more: did M. Halliday make any mention of his plans for the evening?"

"He said nothing whatever, monsieur."

"I thank you, madame, and I apologise for disturbing you. Pray do not trouble—we can find our way out."

We stepped out into the hall. A lady was just entering the front door as we did so. She ran quickly up the stairs, and I was left with an impression of the heavy mourning that denotes a French widow.

"A most unusual type of woman, that," remarked Poirot, as we walked away.

"Madame Olivier? Yes, she—"

"*Mais non,* not Madame Olivier. *Cela va sans dire!* There are not many geniuses of her stamp in the world. No, I referred to the other lady—the lady on the stairs."

"I didn't see her face," I said, staring. "And I hardly see how you could have done. She never looked at us."

"That is why I said she was an unusual type," said Poirot placidly. "A woman who enters her home—for I presume that it is her home since she enters with a key— and runs straight upstairs without even looking at two strange visitors in the hall to see who they are, is a *very* unusual type of woman—quite unnatural, in fact. *Mille tonnerres!* what is that?"

He dragged me back—just in time. A tree had crashed down on to the side walk, just missing us. Poirot stared at it, pale and upset.

"It was a near thing that! But clumsy, all the same— for I had no suspicion—at least hardly any suspicion. Yes, but for my quick eyes, the eyes of a cat, Hercule Poirot might now be crushed out of existence—a terrible calamity for the world. And you, too, *mon ami*—though that would not be such a national catastrophe."

"Thank you," I said coldly. "And what are we going to do now?"

"Do?" cried Poirot. "We are going to think. Yes, here and now, we are going to exercise our little gray cells. This M. Halliday now, was he really in Paris? Yes, for Professor Bourgoneau, who knows him, saw and spoke to him."

"What on earth are you driving at?" I cried.

"That was Friday morning. He was last seen at eleven Friday night—but *was* he seen then?"

"The porter—"

"A night porter—who had not previously seen Halliday. A man comes in, sufficiently like Halliday—we may trust Number Four for that—asks for letters, goes upstairs, packs a small suitcase, and slips out the next morning. Nobody saw Halliday all that evening—no, because he was already in the hands of his enemies. Was it Halliday whom Madame Olivier received? Yes, for though she did not know him by sight, an imposter could hardly deceive her on her own special subject. He came here, he had his interview, he left. What happened next?"

Seizing me by the arm, Poirot was fairly dragging me back to the villa.

"Now, *mon ami*, imagine that it is the day after the disappearance, and that we are tracking footprints. You love footprints, do you not? See—here they go, a man's, Mr. Halliday's. . . . He turns to the right as we did, he walks briskly—ah! other footsteps following behind—very quickly—small footsteps, a woman's. See, she catches him up—a slim young woman, in a widow's veil. 'Pardon, monsieur, Madame Olivier desires that I recall you.' He stops, he turns. Now where would the young woman take him? She does not wish to be seen walking with him. Is it coincidence that she catches up with him just where a narrow alleyway opens, dividing two gardens. She leads him down it. 'It is shorter this way, monsieur.' On the right is the garden of Madame Olivier's villa, on the left the garden of another villa—and from that garden, mark you, the tree fell—so nearly on us. Garden doors from both open on the alley. The ambush is there. Men pour out, overpower him, and carry him into the strange villa."

"Good gracious, Poirot," I cried, "are you pretending to see all this?"

"I see it with the eyes of the mind, *mon ami*. So, and only so, could it have happened. Come, let us go back to the house."

"You want to see Madame Olivier again?"

Poirot gave a curious smile.

"No, Hastings, I want to see the face of the lady on the stairs."

"Who do you think she is, a relation of Madame Olivier's?"

"More probably a secretary—and a secretary engaged not very long ago."

The same gentle acolyte opened the door to us.

"Can you tell me," said Poirot, "the name of the lady, the widow lady, who came in just now?"

"Madame Veroneau? Madame's secretary?"

"That is the lady. Would you be so kind as to ask her to speak to us for a moment."

The youth disappeared. He soon reappeared.

"I am sorry. Madame Veroneau must have gone out again."

"I think not," said Poirot quietly. "Will you give her

my name, M. Hercule Poirot, and say that it is important I should see her at once, as I am just going to the Prefecture."

Again our messenger departed. This time the lady descended. She walked into the salon. We followed her. She turned and raised her veil. To my astonishment I recognised our old antagonist, the Countess Rossakoff, a Russian countess, who had engineered a particularly smart jewel robbery in London.

"As soon as I caught sight of you in the hall, I feared the worst," she observed plaintively.

"My dear Countess Rossakoff—"

She shook her head.

"Inez Véroneau now," she murmured. "A Spaniard, married to a Frenchman. What do you want of me, M. Poirot? You are a terrible man. You hunted me from London. Now, I suppose, you will tell our wonderful Madame Olivier about me, and hunt me from Paris? We poor Russians, we must live, you know."

"It is more serious than that, madame," said Poirot watching her. "I propose to enter the villa next door, and release M. Halliday, if he is still alive. I know everything, you see."

I saw her sudden pallor. She bit her lip. Then she spoke with her usual decision.

"He is still alive—but he is not at the villa. Come, monsieur, I will make a bargain with you. Freedom for me—and M. Halliday, alive and well, for you."

"I accept," said Poirot. "I was about to propose the same bargain myself. By the way, are the Big Four your employers, madame?"

Again I saw that deathly pallor creep over her face, but she left his question unanswered.

Instead, "You permit me to telephone?" she asked, and crossing to the instrument she rang up a number. "The number of the villa," she explained, "where our friend is now imprisoned. You may give it to the police—the nest will be empty when they arrive. Ah! I am through. Is that you, André? It is I, Inez. The little Belgian knows all. Send Halliday to the hotel, and clear out."

She replaced the receiver, and came towards us, smiling.

"You will accompany us to the hotel, madame."

"Naturally. I expected that."

I got a taxi, and we drove off together. I could see by Poirot's face that he was perplexed. The thing was almost too easy. We arrived at the hotel. The porter came up to us.

"A gentleman has arrived. He is in your rooms. He seems very ill. A nurse came with him, but she has left."

"That is all right," said Poirot, "he is a friend of mine."

We went upstairs together. Sitting in a chair by the window was a haggard young fellow who looked in the last stages of exhaustion. Poirot went over to him.

"Are you John Halliday?" The man nodded. "Show me your left arm. John Halliday has a mole just below the left elbow."

The man stretched out his arm. The mole was there. Poirot bowed to the countess. She turned and left the room.

A glass of brandy revived Halliday somewhat.

"My God!" he muttered. "I have been through hell—hell. . . . Those fiends are devils incarnate. My wife, where is she? What does she think? They told me that she would believe—would believe—"

"She does not," said Poirot firmly. "Her faith in you has never wavered. She is waiting for you—she and the child."

"Thank God for that. I can hardly believe that I am free once more."

"Now that you are a little recovered, monsieur, I should like to hear the whole story from the beginning."

Halliday looked at him with an indescribable expression.

"I remember—nothing," he said.

"What?"

"Have you ever heard of the Big Four?"

"Something of them," said Poirot dryly.

"You do not know what I know. They have unlimited power. If I remain silent, I shall be safe—if I say one word—not only I, but my nearest and dearest will suffer unspeakable things. It is no good arguing with me. *I know.* . . . I remember—nothing."

And, getting up, he walked from the room.

Poirot's face wore a baffled expression.

"So it is like that, is it?" he muttered. "The Big Four win again. What is that you are holding in your hand, Hastings?"

I handed it to him.

"The countess scribbled it before she left," I explained.

He read it.

"Au revoir.—I.V."

"Signed with her initials—I.V. Just a coincidence, perhaps, that they also stand for *Four*. I wonder, Hastings, I wonder."

Chapter VII

The Radium Thieves

On the night of his release, Halliday slept in the room next to ours at the hotel, and all night long I heard him moaning and protesting in his sleep. Undoubtedly his experience in the villa had broken his nerve, and in the morning we failed completely to extract any information from him. He would only repeat his statement about the unlimited power at the disposal of the Big Four, and his assurance of the vengeance which would follow if he talked.

After lunch he departed to rejoin his wife in England, but Poirot and I remained behind in Paris. I was all for energetic proceedings of some kind or other, and Poirot's quiescence annoyed me.

"For Heaven's sake, Poirot," I urged, "let us be up and at them."

"Admirable, *mon ami,* admirable! Up where, and at whom? Be precise, I beg of you."

"At the Big Four, of course."

"*Cela va sans dire.* But how would you set about it?"

"The police," I hazarded doubtfully.

Poirot smiled.

"They would accuse us of romancing. We have nothing to go upon—nothing whatever. We must wait."

"Wait for what?"

"Wait for them to make a move. See now, in England you all comprehend and adore *le boxe.* If one man does not make a move, the other must, and by permitting the adversary to make the attack one learns something about him. That is our part—to let the other side make the attack."

"You think they will?" I said doubtfully.

"I have no doubt whatever of it. To begin with, see, they try to get me out of England. That fails. Then, in the Dartmoor affair, we step in and save their victim from the gallows. And yesterday, once again, we interfere with their plans. Assuredly, they will not leave the matter there."

As I reflected on this, there was a knock on the door. Without waiting for a reply, a man stepped into the room and closed the door behind him. He was a tall, thin man, with a slightly hooked nose and a sallow complexion. He wore an overcoat buttoned up to his chin, and a soft hat well pulled down over his eyes.

"Excuse me, gentlemen, for my somewhat unceremonious entry," he said in a soft voice, "but my business is of a rather unorthodox nature."

Smiling, he advanced to the table and sat down by it. I was about to spring up, but Poirot restrained me with a gesture.

"As you say, monsieur, your entry is somewhat unceremonious. Will you kindly state your business?"

"My dear M. Poirot, it is very simple. You have been annoying my friends."

"In what way?"

"Come, come, Monsieur Poirot. You do not seriously ask me that? You know as well as I do."

"It depends, monsieur, upon who these friends of yours are."

Without a word, the man drew from his pocket a cigarette case, and, opening it, took out four cigarettes and tossed them on the table. Then he picked them up and returned them to his case, which he replaced in his pocket.

"Aha!" said Poirot, "so it is like that, is it? And what do your friends suggest?"

"They suggest, monsieur, that you should employ your

talents—your very considerable talents—in the detection of legitimate crime—return to your former avocations, and solve the problems of London society ladies."

"A peaceful programme," said Poirot. "And supposing I do not agree?"

The man made an eloquent gesture.

"We should regret it, of course, exceedingly," he said. "So would all the friends and admirers of the great M. Hercule Poirot. But regrets, however poignant, do not bring a man to life again."

"Put very delicately," said Poirot, nodding his head. "And supposing I—accept?"

"In that case I am empowered to offer you—compensation."

He drew out a pocket-book, and threw ten notes on the table. They were for ten thousand francs each.

"That is merely as a guarantee of our good faith," he said. "Ten times that amount will be paid you."

"Good God," I cried, springing up, "you dare to think—!"

"Sit down, Hastings," said Poirot autocratically. "Subdue your so beautiful and honest nature and sit down. To you, monsieur, I will say this. What is to prevent me ringing up the police and giving you into their custody, whilst my friend here prevents you from escaping?"

"By all means do so if you think it advisable," said our visitor calmly.

"Oh! look here, Poirot," I cried. "I can't stand this. Ring up the police and have done with it."

Rising swiftly, I strode to the door and stood with my back against it.

"It seems the obvious course," murmured Poirot, as though debating with himself.

"But you distrust the obvious, eh?" said our visitor, smiling.

"Go on, Poirot," I urged.

"It will be your responsibility, *mon ami*."

As he lifted the receiver, the man made a sudden, cat-like jump at me. I was ready for him. In another minute we were locked together, staggering round the room. Suddenly I felt him slip and falter. I pressed my advantage. He went down before me. And then, in the very flush of victory, an extraordinary thing happened. I felt myself flying forwards. Head first, I crashed into the wall in a complicated heap. I was up in a minute, but the door was already closing behind my late adversary. I rushed to it and shook it; it was locked on the outside. I seized the telephone from Poirot.

"Is that the bureau? Stop a man who is coming out. A tall man, with a buttoned-up overcoat and a soft hat. He is wanted by the police."

Very few minutes elapsed before we heard a noise in the corridor outside. The key was turned and the door flung open. The manager himself stood in the doorway.

"The man—you have got him?" I cried.

"No, monsieur. No one has descended."

"You must have passed him."

"We have passed no one, monsieur. It is incredible that he can have escaped."

"You have passed some one, I think," said Poirot, in his gentle voice. "One of the hotel staff, perhaps?"

"Only a waiter carrying a tray, monsieur."

"Ah!" said Poirot, in a tone that spoke infinities.

"So that was why he wore his overcoat buttoned up to his chin," mused Poirot, when we had finally got rid of the excited hotel officials.

"I'm awfully sorry, Poirot," I murmured, rather crestfallen. "I thought I'd downed him all right."

"Yes, that was a Japanese trick, I fancy. Do not distress yourself, *mon ami*. All went according to plan—his plan. That is what I wanted."

"What's this?" I cried, pouncing on a brown object that lay on the floor.

It was a slim pocket-book of brown leather, and had

evidently fallen from our visitor's pocket during his struggle with me. It contained two receipted bills in the name of M. Felix Laon, and a folded-up piece of paper which made my heart beat faster. It was a half sheet of note-paper on which a few words were scrawled in pencil but they were words of supreme importance.

"The next meeting of the council will be on Friday at 34 Rue des Echelles at 11 a.m."

It was signed with a big figure 4.

And to-day was Friday, and the clock on the mantelpiece showed the hour to be 10:30.

"My God, what a chance!" I cried. "Fate is playing into our hands. We must start at once though. What stupendous luck."

"So that was why he came," murmured Poirot. "I see it all now."

"See what? Come on, Poirot, don't stay daydreaming there."

Poirot looked at me, and slowly shook his head, smiling as he did so.

" 'Will you walk into my parlour, said the spider to the fly?' That is your little English nursery rhyme, is it not? No, no—they are subtle—but not so subtle as Hercule Poirot."

"What on earth are you driving at, Poirot?"

"My friend, I have been asking myself the reason of this morning's visit. Did our visitor really hope to succeed in bribing me? Or, alternatively, in frightening me into abandoning my task? It seemed hardly credible. Why, then, did he come? And now I see the whole plan—very neat— very pretty—the ostensible reason to bribe or frighten me— the necessary struggle which he took no pains to avoid, and which should make the dropped pocket-book natural and reasonable—and finally—the pitfall! Rue des Echelles, 11 a.m.? I think not, *mon ami*! One does not catch Hercule Poirot as easily as that."

"Good heavens," I gasped.

Poirot was frowning to himself.

"There is still one thing I do not understand."

"What is that?"

"The time, Hastings—the time. If they wanted to decoy me away, surely night time would be better? Why this early hour? Is it possible that something is about to happen this morning? Something which they are anxious Hercule Poirot should not know about?"

He shook his head.

"We shall see. Here I sit, *mon ami*. We do not stir out this morning. We await events here."

It was at half-past eleven exactly that the summons came. A *petit bleu*. Poirot tore it open, then handed it to me. It was from Madame Olivier, the world-famous scientist, whom we had visited yesterday in connection with the Halliday case. It asked us to come out to Passy at once.

We obeyed the summons without an instant's delay. Madame Olivier received us in the same small salon. I was struck anew with the wonderful power of this woman, with her long nun's face and burning eyes—this brilliant successor of Becquerel and the Curies. She came to the point at once.

"Messieurs, you interviewed me yesterday about the disappearance of M. Halliday. I now learn that you returned to the house a second time, and asked to see my secretary, Inez Veroneau. She left the house with you, and has not returned here since."

"Is that all, madame?"

"No, monsieur, it is not. Last night the laboratory was broken into, and several valuable papers and memoranda were stolen. The thieves had a try for something more precious still, but luckily they failed to open the big safe."

"Madame, these are the facts of the case. Your late secretary, Madame Veroneau, was really the Countess Rossakoff, an expert thief, and it was she who was responsible for the disappearance of M. Halliday. How long had she been with you?"

"Five months, monsieur. What you say amazes me."

"It is true, nevertheless. These papers, were they easy to find? Or do you think an inside knowledge was shown?"

"It is rather curious that the thieves knew exactly where to look. You think Inez—"

"Yes, I have no doubt that it was upon her information that they acted. But what is this precious thing that the thieves failed to find? Jewels?"

Madame Olivier shook her head with a faint smile.

"Something much more precious than that, monsieur." She looked round her, then bent forward, lowering her voice. "Radium, monsieur."

"Radium?"

"Yes, monsieur. I am now at the crux of my experiments. I possess a small portion of radium myself—more has been lent to me for the process I am at work upon. Small though the actual quantity is, it comprises a large amount of the world's stock and represents a value of millions of francs."

"And where is it?"

"In its leaden case in the big safe—the safe purposely appears to be of an old and worn-out pattern, but it is really a triumph of the safe-makers' art. That is probably why the thieves were unable to open it."

"How long are you keeping this radium in your possession?"

"Only for two days more, monsieur. Then my experiments will be concluded."

Poirot's eyes brightened.

"And Inez Veroneau is aware of the fact? Good—then our friends will come back. Not a word of me to any one, madame. But rest assured, I will save your radium for you. You have a key of the door leading from the laboratory to the garden?"

"Yes, monsieur. Here it is. I have a duplicate for myself. And here is the key of the garden door leading out into the alleyway between this villa and the next one."

"I thank you, madame. To-night, go to bed as usual, have no fears, and leave all to me. But not a word to any one—not to your two assistants—Mademoiselle Claude and Monsieur Henri, is it not?—particularly not a word to them."

Poirot left the villa rubbing his hands in great satisfaction.

"What are we going to do now?" I asked.

"Now, Hastings, we are about to leave Paris—for England."

"What?"

"We will pack our effects, have lunch, and drive to the Gare du Nord."

"But the radium?"

"I said we were going to leave for England—I did not say we were going to arrive there. Reflect a moment, Hastings. It is quite certain that we are being watched and followed. Our enemies must believe that we are going back to England, and they certainly will not believe that unless they see us get on board the train and start."

"Do you mean we are to slip off again at the last minute?"

"No, Hastings. Our enemies will be satisfied with nothing less than a *bona fide* departure."

"But the train doesn't stop until Calais?"

"It will stop if it is paid to do so."

"Oh, come now, Poirot—surely you can't pay an express to stop—they'd refuse."

"My dear friend, have you never remarked the little handle—the *signale d'arrêt*—penalty for improper use, 100 francs, I think?"

"Oh! you are going to pull that?"

"Or rather a friend of mine, Pierre Combeau, will do so. Then, while he is arguing with the guard, and making a big scene, and all the train is agog with interest, you and I will fade quietly away."

We duly carried out Poirot's plan. Pierre Combeau, an

old crony of Poirot's, and who evidently knew my little friend's methods pretty well, fell in with the arrangements. The communication cord was pulled just as we got to the outskirts of Paris. Combeau "made a scene" in the most approved French fashion and Poirot and I were able to leave the train without any one being interested in our departure. Our first proceeding was to make a considerable change in our appearance. Poirot had brought the materials for this with him in a small case. Two loafers in dirty blue blouses were the result. We had dinner in an obscure hostelry, and started back to Paris afterwards.

It was close on eleven o'clock when we found ourselves once more in the neighbourhood of Madame Olivier's villa. We looked up and down the road before slipping into the alleyway. The whole place appeared to be perfectly deserted. One thing we could be quite certain of, no one was following us.

"I do not expect them to be here yet," whispered Poirot to me. "Possibly they may not come until to-morrow night, but they know perfectly well that there are only two nights on which the radium will be there."

Very cautiously we turned the key in the garden door. It opened noiselessly and we stepped into the garden.

And then, with complete unexpectedness, the blow fell. In a minute we were surrounded, gagged and bound. At least ten men must have been waiting for us. Resistance was useless. Like two helpless bundles we were lifted up and carried along. To my intense astonishment, they took us *towards* the house and not away from it. With a key they opened the door into the laboratory and carried us into it. One of the men stooped down before the big safe. The door of it swung open. I felt an unpleasant sensation down my spine. Were they going to bundle us into it, and leave us there to asphyxiate slowly?

However, to my amazement, I saw that from the inside of the safe steps led down beneath the floor. We were thrust down this narrow way and eventually came out into a big subterranean chamber. A woman stood there, tall and imposing, with a black velvet mask covering her face. She was clearly in command of the situation by her gestures of authority. The men slung us down on the floor and left us—alone with the mysterious creature in the mask. I had no doubt who she was. This was the unknown French-woman—Number Three of the Big Four.

She knelt down beside us and removed the gags, but left us bound, then rising and facing us, with a sudden swift gesture she removed her mask.

It was Madame Olivier!

"M. Poirot," she said, in a low mocking tone. "The great, the wonderful, the unique M. Poirot. I sent a warning to you yesterday morning. You chose to disregard it—you thought you could pit your wits against US. And now, you are here!"

There was a cold malignity about her that froze me to the marrow. It was so at variance with the burning fire of her eyes. She was mad—mad—with the madness of genius!

Poirot said nothing. His jaw had dropped, and he was staring at her.

"Well," she said softly, "this is the end. WE cannot permit our plans to be interfered with. Have you any last request to make?"

Never before, or since, have I felt so near death. Poirot was magnificent. He neither flinched nor paled, just stared at her with unabated interest.

"Your psychology interests me enormously, madame," he said quietly. "It is a pity that I have so short a time to devote to studying it. Yes, I have a request to make. A condemned man is always allowed a last smoke, I believe. I have my cigarette case on me. If you would permit—" He looked down at his bonds.

"Ah, yes!" she laughed. "You would like me to untie your hands, would you not? You are clever, M. Hercule Poirot, I know that. I shall not untie your hands—but I will find you a cigarette."

She knelt down by him, extracted his cigarette case, took out a cigarette, and placed it between his lips.

"And now a match," she said, rising.

"It is not necessary, madame." Something in his voice startled me. She, too, was arrested.

"Do not move, I pray of you, madame. You will regret it if you do. Are you acquainted at all with the properties of curare? The South American Indians use it as an arrow poison. A scratch with it means death. Some tribes use a little blow-pipe—I, too, have a little blow-pipe constructed so as to look exactly like a cigarette. I have only to blow. . . . Ah! you start. Do not move, madame. The mechanism of this cigarette is most ingenious. One blows—and a tiny dart resembling a fishbone flies through the air—to find its mark. You do not wish to die, madame. Therefore, I beg of you, release my friend Hastings from his bonds. I cannot use my hands, but I can turn my head—so—you are still covered, madame. Make no mistake, I beg of you."

Slowly, with shaking hands, and rage and hate convulsing her face, she bent down and did his bidding. I was free. Poirot's voice gave me instructions.

"Your bonds will now do for the lady, Hastings. That is right. Is she securely fastened? Then release me, I pray of you. It is a fortunate circumstance she sent away her henchmen. With a little luck we may hope to find the way out unobstructed."

In another minute, Poirot stood by my side. He bowed to the lady.

"Hercule Poirot is not killed so easily, madame. I wish you good-night."

The gag prevented her from replying, but the murderous gleam in her eyes frightened me. I hoped devoutly that we should never fall into her power again.

Three minutes later we were outside the villa, and hurriedly traversing the garden. The road outside was deserted, and we were soon clear of the neighbourhood.

Then Poirot broke out.

"I deserve all that that woman said to me. I am a triple imbecile, a miserable animal, thirty-six times an idiot. I was proud of myself for not falling into their trap. And it was not even meant as a trap—except exactly in the way in which I fell into it. They knew I would see through it— they counted on my seeing through it. This explains all— the ease with which they surrendered Halliday—everything. Madame Olivier was the ruling spirit—Vera Rossakoff only her lieutenant. Madame needed Halliday's ideas—she herself had the necessary genius to supply the gaps that perplexed him. Yes, Hastings, we know now who Number Three is—the woman who is probably the greatest scientist in the world! Think of it. The brain of the East, the science of the West—and two others whose identities we do not yet know. But we must find out. To-morrow we will return to London and set about it."

"You are not going to denounce Madame Olivier to the police?"

"I should not be believed. That woman is one of the idols of France. And we can prove nothing. We are lucky if she does not denounce us."

"What?"

"Think of it. We are found at night upon the premises with keys in our possession which she will swear she never gave us. She surprises us at the safe, and we gag and bind her and make away. Have no illusions, Hastings. The boot is not upon the right leg—is that how you say it?"

Chapter VIII

In the House of the Enemy

AFTER our adventure in the villa at Passy, we returned post haste to London. Several letters were awaiting Poirot. He read one of them with a curious smile, and then handed it to me.

"Read this, *mon ami.*"

I turned first to the signature, "Abe Ryland," and recalled Poirot's words: "the richest man in the world." Mr. Ryland's letter was curt and incisive. He expressed himself as profoundly dissatisfied with the reasons Poirot had given for withdrawing from the South American proposition at the last moment.

"This gives one furiously to think, does it not?" said Poirot.

"I suppose it's only natural he should be a bit ratty."

"No, no, you comprehend not. Remember the words of Mayerling, the man who took refuge here—only to die by the hands of his enemies. 'Number Two is represented by an "S" with two lines through it—the sign for a dollar, also by two stripes and a star. It may be conjectured therefore that he is an American subject, and that he represents the power of wealth.' Add to those words the fact that Ryland offered me a huge sum to tempt me out of England—and—and what about it, Hastings?"

"You mean," I said, staring, "that you suspect Abe

Ryland, the multi-millionaire, of being Number Two of the Big Four."

"Your bright intellect has grasped the idea, Hastings. Yes, I do. The tone in which you said multi-millionaire was eloquent—but let me impress upon you one fact—this thing is being run by men at the top—and Mr. Ryland has the reputation of being no beauty in his business dealings. An able, unscrupulous man, a man who has all the wealth that he needs, and is out for unlimited power."

There was undoubtedly something to be said for Poirot's view. I asked him when he had made up his mind definitely upon the point.

"That is just it. I am not sure. I cannot be sure. *Mon ami*, I would give anything to *know*. Let me but place Number Two definitely as Abe Ryland, and we draw nearer to our goal."

"He has just arrived in London, I see by this," I said, tapping the letter. "Shall you call upon him, and make your apologies in person?"

"I might do so."

Two days later, Poirot returned to our rooms in a state of boundless excitement. He grasped me by both hands in his most impulsive manner.

"My friend, an occasion stupendous, unprecedented, never to be repeated, has presented itself! But there is danger, grave danger. I should not even ask you to attempt it."

If Poirot was trying to frighten me, he was going the wrong way to work, and so I told him. Becoming less incoherent, he unfolded his plan.

It seemed that Ryland was looking for an English secretary, one with a good social manner and presence. It was Poirot's suggestion that I should apply for the post.

"I would do it, myself, *mon ami*," he explained apologetically. "But, see you, it is almost impossible for me to disguise myself in the needful manner. I speak the English very well—except when I am excited—but hardly so as to deceive the ear; and even though I were to sacrifice my moustaches, I doubt not but that I should still be recognisable as Hercule Poirot."

I doubted it also, and declared myself ready and willing to take up the part and penetrate into Ryland's household.

"Ten to one he won't engage me anyway," I remarked.

"Oh, yes, he will. I will arrange for you such testimonials as shall make him lick his lips. The Home Secretary himself shall recommend you."

This seemed to be carrying things a bit far, but Poirot waved aside my remonstrances.

"Oh, yes, he will do it. I investigated for him a little matter which might have caused a grave scandal. All was solved with discretion and delicacy, and now, as you would say, he perches upon my hand like the little bird and pecks the crumbs."

Our first step was to engage the services of an artist in "makeup." He was a little man, with a quaint bird-like turn of the head, not unlike Poirot's own. He considered me some time in silence, and then fell to work. When I looked at myself in the glass half an hour afterwards, I was amazed. Special shoes caused me to stand at least two inches taller, and the coat I wore was arranged so as to give me a long, lank, weedy look. My eyebrows had been cunningly altered, giving a totally different expression to my face, I wore pads in my cheeks, and the deep tan of my face was a thing of the past. My moustache had gone, and a gold tooth was prominent on one side of my mouth.

"Your name," said Poirot, "is Arthur Neville. God guard you, my friend—for I fear that you go into perilous places."

It was with a beating heart that I presented myself at the Savoy, at an hour named by Mr. Ryland, and asked to see the great man.

After being kept waiting a minute or two, I was shown upstairs to his suite.

Ryland was sitting at a table. Spread out in front of him was a letter which I could see out of the tail of my eye was in the Home Secretary's handwriting. It was my first sight of the American millionaire, and, in spite of myself, I was impressed. He was tall and lean, with a jutting out chin and slightly hooked nose. His eyes glittered cold and gray behind penthouse brows. He had thick grizzled hair, and a long black cigar (without which, I learned later, he was never seen) protruded rakishly from the corner of his mouth.

"Siddown," he grunted.

I sat. He tapped the letter in front of him.

"According to this piece here, you're the goods all right, and I don't need to look further. Say, are you well up in the social matters?"

I said that I thought I could satisfy him in that respect.

"I mean to say, if I have a lot of dooks and earls and viscounts and suchlike down to the country place I've gotten, you'll be able to sort them out all right and put them where they should be round the dining table?"

"Oh! quite easily," I replied, smiling.

We exchanged a few more preliminaries, and then I found myself engaged. What Mr. Ryland wanted was a secretary conversant with English society, as he already had an American secretary and a stenographer with him.

Two days later I went down to Hatton Chase, the seat of the Duke of Loamshire, which the American millionaire had rented for a period of six months.

My duties gave me no difficulty whatever. At one period of my life I had been private secretary to a busy member of Parliament, so I was not called upon to assume a role unfamiliar to me. Mr. Ryland usually entertained a large party over the week-end, but the middle of the week was comparatively quiet. I saw very little of Mr. Appleby, the American secretary, but he seemed a pleasant, normal young American, very efficient in his work. Of Miss Martin, the stenographer, I saw rather more. She was a pretty girl of about twenty-three or four, with auburn hair and brown eyes that could look mischievous enough upon occasion, though they were usually cast demurely down. I had an idea that she both disliked and distrusted her employer, though, of course, she was careful never to hint at anything of the kind, but the time came when I was unexpectedly taken into her confidence.

I had, of course, carefully scrutinised all the members of the household. One or two of the servants had been newly engaged, one of the footmen, I think, and some of the housemaids. The butler, the housekeeper, and the chef were the duke's own staff, who had consented to remain on in the establishment. The housemaids I dismissed as unimportant; I scrutinised James, the second footman, very carefully; but it was clear that he was an under-footman and an under-footman only. He had, indeed, been engaged by the butler. A person of whom I was far more suspicious was Deaves, Ryland's valet, whom he had brought over from New York with him. An Englishman by birth, with an irreproachable manner, I yet harboured vague suspicions about him.

I had been at Hatton Chase three weeks, and not an incident of any kind had arisen which I could lay my finger on in support of our theory. There was no trace of the activities of the Big Four. Mr. Ryland was a man of overpowering force and personality, but I was coming to believe that Poirot had made a mistake when he associated him with that dread organisation. I even heard him mention Poirot in a casual way at dinner one night.

"Wonderful little man, they say. But he's a quitter. How do I know? I put him on a deal, and he turned me down at the last minute. I'm not taking any more of your Monsieur Hercule Poirot."

It was at moments such as these that I felt my cheek pads most wearisome!

And then Miss Martin told me a rather curious story. Ryland had gone to London for the day, taking Appleby with him. Miss Martin and I were strolling together in the garden after tea. I liked the girl very much, she was so unaffected and so natural. I could see that there was something on her mind, and at last out it came.

"Do you know, Major Neville," she said, "I am really thinking of resigning my post here."

I looked somewhat astonished, and she went on hurriedly.

"Oh! I know it's a wonderful job to have got, in a way. I suppose most people would think me a fool to throw it up. But I can't stand abuse, Major Neville. To be sworn at like a trooper is more than I can bear. No gentleman would do such a thing."

"Has Ryland been swearing at you?"

She nodded.

"Of course, he's always rather irritable and short-tempered. That one expects. It's all in the day's work. But to fly into such an absolute fury—over nothing at all. He really looked as though he could have murdered me! And, as I say, over nothing at all!"

"Tell me about it?" I said, keenly interested.

"As you know, I open all Mr. Ryland's letters. Some I hand on to Mr. Appleby, others I deal with myself, but I do all the preliminary sorting. Now there are certain letters that come, written on blue paper, and with a tiny 4 marked on the corner—I beg your pardon, did you speak?"

I had been unable to repress a stifled exclamation, but I hurriedly shook my head, and begged her to continue.

"Well, as I was saying, these letters come, and there are strict orders that they are never to be opened, but to be handed over to Mr. Ryland intact. And, of course, I always do so. But there was an unusually heavy mail yesterday morning, and I was opening the letters in a terrific hurry. By mistake I opened one of these letters. As soon as I saw what I had done, I took it to Mr. Ryland and explained. To my utter amazement he flew into the most awful rage. As I tell you, I was quite frightened."

"What was there in the letter, I wonder, to upset him so?"

"Absolutely nothing—that's just the curious part of it. I had read it before I discovered my mistake. It was quite short. I can still remember it word for word, and there was nothing in it that could possibly upset any one."

"You can repeat it, you say?" I encouraged her.

"Yes." She paused a minute and then repeated slowly, whilst I noted down the words unobtrusively, the following:—

"DEAR SIR,—The essential thing now, I should say, is to see the property. If you insist on the quarry being included, then seventeen thousand seems reasonable. 11% commission too much, 4% is ample.

"Yours truly,

"ARTHUR LEVERSHAM."

Miss Martin went on:—

"Evidently about some property Mr. Ryland was thinking of buying. But really, I do feel that a man who can get into a rage over such a trifle is, well, dangerous. What do you think I ought to do, Major Neville? You've more experience of the world than I have."

I soothed the girl down, pointed out to her that Mr. Ryland had probably been suffering from the enemy of his race—dyspepsia. In the end I sent her away quite comforted. But I was not so easily satisfied myself. When the girl had gone, and I was alone, I took out my notebook, and ran over the letter which I had jotted down. What did it mean—this apparently innocent-sounding missive? Did it concern some business deal which Ryland was undertaking, and was he anxious that no details about it should leak out until it was carried through? That was a possible explanation. But I remembered the small figure 4 with which the envelopes were marked, and I felt that, at last, I was on the track of the thing we were seeking.

I puzzled over the letter all that evening, and most of the next day—and then suddenly the solution came to me. It was so simple, too. The figure 4 was the clue. Read every fourth word in the letter, and an entirely different message appeared. "Essential should see you quarry seventeen eleven four."

The solution of the figures was easy. Seventeen stood for the seventeenth of October—which was to-morrow, eleven was the time, and four was the signature—either referring to the mysterious Number Four himself—or else it was the "trade-mark" so to speak, of the Big Four. The quarry was also intelligible. There was a big disused quarry on the estate about half a mile from the house—a lonely spot, ideal for a secret meeting.

For a moment or two I was tempted to run the show myself. It would be such a feather in my cap, for once, to have the pleasure of crowing over Poirot.

But in the end I overcame the temptation. This was a big business—I had no right to play a lone hand, and perhaps jeopardise our chances of success. For the first time, we had stolen a march upon our enemies. We must make good this time—and, disguise the fact as I might, Poirot had the better brain of the two.

I wrote off posthaste to him, laying the facts before him, and explaining how urgent it was that we should overhear what went on at the interview. If he liked to leave it to me, well and good, but I gave him detailed instructions how to reach the quarry from the station in case he should deem it wise to be present himself.

I took the letter down to the village and posted it myself. I had been able to communicate with Poirot throughout my stay, by the simple expedient of posting my letters myself, but we had agreed that he should not attempt to communicate with me in case my letters should be tampered with.

I was in a glow of excitement the following evening. No guests were staying in the house, and I was busy with

Mr. Ryland in his study all the evening. I had foreseen that this would be the case, which was why I had had no hope of being able to meet Poirot at the station. I was, however, confident that I would be dismissed well before eleven o'clock.

Sure enough, just after ten-thirty, Mr. Ryland glanced at the clock, and announced that he was "through." I took the hint and retired discreetly. I went upstairs as though going to bed, but slipped quietly down a side staircase and let myself out into the garden, having taken the precaution to don a dark overcoat to hide my white shirt-front.

I had gone some way down the garden when I chanced to look over my shoulder. Mr. Ryland was just stepping out from his study window into the garden. He was starting to keep the appointment. I redoubled my pace, so as to get a clear start. I arrived at the quarry somewhat out of breath. There seemed no one about, and I crawled into a thick tangle of bushes and awaited developments.

Ten minutes later, just on the stroke of eleven, Ryland stalked up, his hat over his eyes and the inevitable cigar in his mouth. He gave a quick look round, and then plunged into the hollows of the quarry below. Presently I heard a low murmur of voices come up to me. Evidently the other man—or men—whoever they were, had arrived first at the rendezvous. I crawled cautiously out of the bushes, and inch by inch, using the utmost precaution against noise, I wormed myself down the steep path. Only a boulder now separated me from the talking men. Secure in the blackness, I peeped round the edge of it and found myself facing the muzzle of a black, murderous-looking automatic!

"Hands up!" said Mr. Ryland succinctly. "I've been waiting for you."

He was seated in the shadow of the rock, so that I could not see his face, but the menace in his voice was unpleasant. Then I felt a ring of cold steel on the back of my neck, and Ryland lowered his own automatic.

"That's right, George," he drawled. "March him around here."

Raging inwardly, I was conducted to a spot in the shadows, where the unseen George (whom I suspected of being the impeccable Deaves), gagged and bound me securely.

Ryland spoke again in a tone which I had difficulty in recognising, so cold and menacing was it.

"This is going to be the end of you two. You've got in the way of the Big Four once too often. Ever heard of land slides? There was one about here two years ago. There's going to be another to-night. I've fixed that good and square. Say, that friend of yours doesn't keep his dates very punctually."

A wave of horror swept over me. Poirot! In another minute he would walk straight into the trap. And I was powerless to warn him. I could only pray that he had elected to leave the matter in my hands, and had remained in London. Surely, if he had been coming, he would have been here by now.

With every minute that passed, my hopes rose.

Suddenly they were dashed to pieces. I heard foot-steps—cautious footsteps, but footsteps nevertheless. I writhed in impotent agony. They came down the path, paused, and then Poirot himself appeared, his head a little on one side, peering into the shadows.

I heard the growl of satisfaction Ryland gave as he raised the big automatic and shouted, "Hands up." Deaves sprang forward as he did so, and took Poirot in the rear. The ambush was complete.

"Pleased to meet you, Mr. Hercule Poirot," said the American grimly.

Poirot's self-possession was marvellous. He did not turn a hair. But I saw his eyes searching in the shadows.

"My friend? He is here?"

"Yes, you are both in the trap—the trap of the Big Four."

He laughed.

"A trap?" queried Poirot.

"Say, haven't you tumbled to it yet?"

"I comprehend that there is a trap—yes," said Poirot gently. "But you are in error, monsieur. It is *you* who are in it—not I and my friend."

"What?" Ryland raised the big automatic, but I saw his gaze falter.

"If you fire, you commit murder watched by ten pairs of eyes, and you will be hanged for it. This place is surrounded—has been for the last hour—by Scotland Yard men. It is checkmate, Mr. Abe Ryland."

He uttered a curious whistle, and as though by magic, the place was alive with men. They seized Ryland and the valet and disarmed them. After speaking a few words to the officer in charge, Poirot took me by the arm, and led me away.

Once clear of the quarry he embraced me with vigour.

"You are alive—you are unhurt. It is magnificent. Often have I blamed myself for letting you go."

"I'm perfectly all right," I said, disengaging myself. "But I'm just a big fogged. You tumbled to their little scheme, did you?"

"But I was waiting for it! For what else did I permit you to go there? Your false name, your disguise, not for a moment was it intended to deceive!"

"What?" I cried. "You never told me."

"As I have frequently told you, Hastings, you have a nature so beautiful and so honest that unless you are yourself deceived, it is impossible for you to deceive others. Good, then, you are spotted from the first, and they do what I had counted on their doing—a mathematical certainty to any one who uses his gray cells properly—use you as a decoy. They set the girl on— By the way, *mon ami,* as an interesting fact psychologically, has she got red hair?"

"If you mean Miss Martin," I said coldly, "her hair is a delicate shade of auburn, but—"

"They are *épatant*—these people! They have even studied your psychology. Oh! yes, my friend, Miss Martin was in the plot—very much so. She repeats the letter to you, together with her tale of Mr. Ryland's wrath, you write it down, you puzzle your brains—the cipher is nicely arranged, difficult, but not too difficult—you solve it, and you send for me.

"But what they do not know is that I am waiting for just this very thing to happen. I go posthaste to Japp and arrange things. And so, as you see, all is triumph!"

I was not particularly pleased with Poirot, and I told him so. We went back to London on a milk train in the early hours of the morning, and a most uncomfortable journey it was.

I was just out of my bath and indulging in pleasurable thoughts of breakfast when I heard Japp's voice in the sitting-room. I threw on a bathrobe and hurried in.

"A pretty mare's nest you've got us into this time," Japp was saying. "It's too bad of you, M. Poirot. First time I've ever known you take a toss."

Poirot's face was a study. Japp went on.

"There were we, taking all this Black Hand stuff seriously—and all the time it was the footman."

"The footman?" I gasped.

"Yes, James, or whatever his name is. Seems he laid 'em a wager in the servants' hall that he could get taken for the old man by his nibs—that's you, Captain Hastings—and would hand him out a lot of spy stuff about a Big Four gang."

"Impossible!" I cried.

"Don't you believe it. I marched our gentleman straight to Hatton Chase, and there was the real Ryland in bed and asleep, and the butler and the cook and God knows how many of them to swear to the wager. Just a silly hoax—that's all it was—and the valet is with him."

"So that was why he kept in the shadow," murmured Poirot.

After Japp had gone we looked at each other.

"We *know*, Hastings," said Poirot at last. "Number Two of the Big Four is Abe Ryland. The masquerading on the part of the footman was to ensure a way of retreat in case of emergencies. And the footman—"

"Yes," I breathed.

"Number Four," said Poirot gravely.

CHAPTER IX

THE YELLOW JASMINE MYSTERY

IT was all very well for Poirot to say that we were acquiring information all the time and gaining an insight into our adversaries' minds—I felt myself that I required some more tangible success than this.

Since we had come into contact with the Big Four, they had committed two murders, abducted Halliday, and had been within an ace of killing Poirot and myself; whereas so far we had hardly scored a point in the game.

Poirot treated my complaints lightly.

"So far, Hastings," he said, "they laugh. That is true, but you have a proverb, have you not: 'He laughs best who laughs at the end'? And at the end, *mon ami,* you shall see.

"You must remember, too," he added, "that we deal with no ordinary criminal, but with the second greatest brain in the world."

I forbore to pander to his conceit by asking the obvious question. I knew the answer, at least I knew what Poirot's answer would be, and instead I tried without success to elicit some information as to what steps he was taking to track down the enemy. As usual he had kept me completely in the dark as to his movements, but I gathered that he was in touch with secret service agents in India, China, and Russia, and, from his occasional bursts of self-glorification, that he was at least progressing in his favourite game of gauging his enemy's mind.

He had abandoned his private practice almost entirely, and I know that at this time he refused some remarkably handsome fees. True, he would sometimes investigate cases which intrigued him, but he usually dropped them the moment he was convinced that they had no connection with the activities of the Big Four.

This attitude of his was remarkably profitable to our friend, Inspector Japp. Undeniably he gained much kudos for solving several problems in which his success was really due to a half-contemptuous hint from Poirot.

In return for such service Japp supplied full details of any case which he thought might interest the little Belgian, and when he was put in charge of what the newspaper called "The Yellow Jasmine Mystery," he wired Poirot, asking him whether he would care to come down and look into the case.

It was in response to this wire that, about a month after my adventure in Abe Ryland's house, we found ourselves alone in a railway compartment whirling away from the smoke and dust of London, bound for the little town of Market Handford in Worcestershire, the seat of the mystery.

Poirot leant back in his corner.

"And what exactly is your opinion of the affair, Hastings?"

I did not at once reply to his question; I felt the need of going warily.

"It all seems so complicated," I said cautiously.

"Does it not?" said Poirot delightedly.

"I suppose our rushing off like this is a pretty clear sign that you consider Mr. Paynter's death to be murder— not suicide or the result of an accident?"

"No, no; you misunderstand me, Hastings. Granting that Mr. Paynter died as the result of a particularly terrible accident, there are still a number of mysterious circumstances to be explained."

"That was what I meant when I said it was all so complicated."

"Let us go over all the main facts quietly and methodically. Recount them to me, Hastings, in an orderly and lucid fashion."

I started forthwith, endeavouring to be as orderly and lucid as I could.

"We start," I said, "with Mr. Paynter. A man of fifty-five, rich, cultured, and somewhat of a globe-trotter. For the last twelve years he has been little in England, but suddenly tiring of incessant travelling, he bought a small place in Worcestershire, near Market Handford, and prepared to settle down. His first action was to write to his only relative, a nephew, Gerald Paynter, the son of his younger brother, and to suggest to him that he should come and make his home at Croftlands (as the place is called) with his uncle. Gerald Paynter, who is an impecunious young artist, was glad enough to fall in with the arrangement, and had been living with his uncle for about seven months when the tragedy occurred."

"Your narrative style is masterly," murmured Poirot. "I say to myself, it is a book that talks, not my friend Hastings."

Paying no attention to Poirot, I went on, warming to the story.

"Mr. Paynter kept up a fair staff at Croftlands—six servants as well as his own Chinese body servant—Ah Ling."

"His Chinese servant, Ah Ling," murmured Poirot.

"On Tuesday last, Mr. Paynter complained of feeling unwell after dinner, and one of the servants was despatched to fetch the doctor. Mr. Paynter received the doctor in his study, having refused to go to bed. What passed between them was not then known, but before Doctor Quentin left, he asked to see the housekeeper, and mentioned that he had given Mr. Paynter a hypodermic injection as his heart was in a very weak state, recommended that he should not be disturbed, and then proceeded to ask some rather curious questions about the servants—how long they had been there, from whom they had come, etc.

"The housekeeper answered these questions as best she could, but was rather puzzled as to their purport. A terrible discovery was made on the following morning. One of the housemaids, on descending, was met by a sickening odour of burned flesh which seemed to come from her master's study. She tried the door, but it was locked on the inside. With the assistance of Gerald Paynter and the Chinaman that was soon broken in, but a terrible sight greeted them. Mr. Paynter had fallen forward into the gas fire, and his face and head were charred beyond recognition.

"Of course, at the moment, no suspicion was aroused as to its being anything but a ghastly accident. If blame attached to any one, it was to Doctor Quentin for giving his patient a narcotic and leaving him in such a dangerous position. And then a rather curious discovery was made.

"There was a newspaper on the floor, lying where it had slipped from the old man's knees. On turning it over, words were found to be scrawled across it, feebly traced in ink. A writing-table stood close to the chair in which Mr. Paynter had been sitting, and the forefinger of the victim's right hand was ink-stained up to the second joint. It was clear that, too weak to hold a pen, Mr. Paynter had dipped his finger in the ink-pot and managed to scrawl these two words across the surface of the newspaper he held—but the words themselves seemed utterly fantastic: *Yellow Jasmine*—just that and nothing more.

"Croftlands has a large quantity of yellow jasmine growing up its walls, and it was thought that this dying message had some reference to them, showing that the poor old man's mind was wandering. Of course, the newspapers, agog for anything out of the common, took up the story hotly, calling it the Mystery of the Yellow Jasmine—though in all probability the words are completely unimportant."

"They are unimportant, you say?" said Poirot. "Well, doubtless, since you say so, it must be so."

I regarded him dubiously, but I could detect no mockery in his eye.

"And then," I continued, "there came the excitements of the inquest."

"This is where you lick your lips, I perceive."

"There was a certain amount of feeling evidenced against Dr. Quentin. To begin with, he was not the regular doctor, only a locum, putting in a month's work, whilst Dr. Bolitho was away on a well-earned holiday. Then it was felt that his carelessness was the direct cause of the accident. But his evidence was little short of sensational. Mr. Paynter had been ailing in health ever since his arrival at Croftlands. Dr. Bolitho had attended him for some time, but when Dr. Quentin first saw his patient, he was mystified by some of the symptoms. He had only attended him once before the night when he was sent for after dinner. As soon as he was alone with Mr. Paynter, the latter had unfolded a surprising tale. To begin with, he was not feeling ill at all, he explained, but the taste of some curry that he had been eating at dinner had struck him as peculiar. Making an excuse to get rid of Ah Ling for a few minutes, he had turned the contents of his plate into a bowl, and he now handed it over to the doctor with injunction to find out if there were really anything wrong with it.

"In spite of his statement that he was not feeling ill, the doctor noted that the shock of his suspicions had evidently affected him, and that his heart was feeling it. Accordingly he administered an injection—not of a narcotic, but of strychnine.

"That, I think, completes the case—except for *the* crux of the whole thing—the fact that the uneaten curry, duly analysed, was found to contain enough powdered opium to have killed two men!"

I paused.

"And your conclusions, Hastings?" asked Poirot quietly.

"It's difficult to say. It *might* be an accident—the fact

that some one attempted to poison him the same night might be merely a coincidence."

"But you don't think so? You prefer to believe it—murder!"

"Don't you?"

"*Mon ami,* you and I do not reason in the same way. I am not trying to make up my mind between two opposite solutions—murder or accident—that will come when we have solved the other problem—the mystery of the 'Yellow Jasmine.' By the way, you have left out something there."

"You mean the two lines at right angles to each other faintly indicated under the words? I did not think they could be of any possible importance."

"What you think is always so important to yourself, Hastings. But let us pass from the mystery of the Yellow Jasmine to the Mystery of the Curry."

"I know. Who poisoned it? Why? There are a hundred questions one can ask. Ah Ling, of course, prepared it. But why should he wish to kill his master? Is he a member of a *tong*, or something like that? One reads of such things. The *tong* of the Yellow Jasmine, perhaps. Then there is Gerald Paynter."

I came to an abrupt pause.

"Yes," said Poirot, nodding his head. "There is Gerald Paynter, as you say. He is his uncle's heir. He was dining out that night, though."

"He might have got at some of the ingredients of the curry," I suggested. "And he would take care to be out, so as not to have to partake of the dish."

I think my reasoning rather impressed Poirot. He looked at me with a more respectful attention than he had given me so far.

"He returns late," I mused, pursuing a hypothetical case. "Sees the light in his uncle's study, enters, and, finding his plan has failed, thrusts the old man down into the fire."

"Mr. Paynter, who was a fairly hearty man of fifty-five, would not permit himself to be burnt to death without a struggle, Hastings. Such a reconstruction is not feasible."

"Well, Poirot," I cried, "we're nearly there, I fancy. Let us hear what you think?"

Poirot threw me a smile, swelled out his chest, and began in a pompous manner.

"Assuming murder, the question at once arises, why choose that particular method? I can think of only one reason—to confuse identity, the face being charred beyond recognition."

"What?" I cried. "You think—"

"A moment's patience, Hastings. I was going on to say that I examine that theory. Is there any ground for believing that the body is not that of Mr. Paynter? Is there any one else whose body it possibly could be? I examine these two questions and finally I answer them both in the negative."

"Oh!" I said, rather disappointed. "And then?"

Poirot's eyes twinkled a little.

"And then I say to myself, 'Since there is here something that I do not understand, it would be well that I should investigate the matter. I must not permit myself to be wholly engrossed by the Big Four.' Ah! we are just arriving. My little clothes brush, where does it hide itself? Here it is—brush me down, I pray you, my friend, and then I will perform the same service for you."

"Yes," said Poirot thoughtfully, as he put away the brush, "one must not permit oneself to be obsessed by one idea. I have been in danger of that. Figure to yourself, my friend, that even here, in this case, I am in danger of it. Those two lines you mentioned, a downstroke and a line at right angles to it, what are they but the beginning of a 4?"

"Good gracious, Poirot," I cried, laughing.

"Is it not absurd? I see the hand of the Big Four everywhere. It is well to employ one's wits in a totally different *milieu*. Ah! there is Japp come to meet us."

CHAPTER X

WE INVESTIGATE AT CROFTLANDS

THE Scotland Yard Inspector was, indeed, waiting on the platform, and greeted us warmly.

"Well, Moosior Poirot, this is good. Thought you'd like to be let in on this. Tip-top mystery, isn't it?"

I read this aright as showing Japp to be completely puzzled and hoping to pick up a pointer from Poirot.

Japp had a car waiting, and we drove up in it to Croftlands. It was a square, white house, quite unpretentious, and covered with creepers, including the starry yellow jasmine. Japp looked up at it as we did.

"Must have been balmy to go writing that, poor old cove," he remarked. "Hallucinations, perhaps, and thought he was outside."

Poirot was smiling at him.

"Which was it, my good Japp?" he asked; "accident or murder?"

The Inspector seemed a little embarrassed by the question.

"Well, if it weren't for that curry business, I'd be for accident every time. There's no sense in holding a live man's head in the fire—why, he'd scream the house down."

"Ah!" said Poirot in a low voice. "Fool that I have been. Triple imbecile! You are a cleverer man than I am, Japp."

Japp was rather taken aback by the compliment—Poirot being usually given to exclusive self-praise. He reddened and muttered something about there being a lot of doubt about that.

He led the way through the house to the room where the tragedy had occurred—Mr. Paynter's study. It was a wide, low room, with book-lined walls and big leather arm-chairs.

Poirot looked across at once to the window which gave upon a gravelled terrace.

"The window, it was unlatched?" he asked.

"That's the whole point, of course. When the doctor left this room, he merely closed the door behind him. The next morning it was found locked. Who locked it? Mr. Paynter? Ah Ling declares that the window was closed and bolted. Dr. Quentin, on the other hand, has an impression that it was closed, but not fastened, but he won't swear either way. If he could, it would make a great difference. If the man *was* murdered, some one entered the room either through the door or the window—if through the door, it was an inside job; if through the window, it might have been any one. First thing when they had broken the door down, they flung the window open, and the housemaid who did it thinks that it wasn't fastened, but she's a precious bad witness—will remember anything you ask her to!"

"What about the key?"

"There you are again. It was on the floor among the wreckage of the door. Might have fallen from the keyhole, might have been dropped there by one of the people who entered, might have been slipped underneath the door from the outside."

"In fact everything is 'might have been'?"

"You've hit it, Moosior Poirot. That's just what it is."

Poirot was looking round him, frowning unhappily.

"I cannot see light," he murmured. "Just now—yes, I got a gleam, but now all is darkness once more. I have not the clue—the motive."

"Young Gerald Paynter had a pretty good motive,"

remarked Japp grimly. "He's been wild enough in his time, I can tell you. *And* extravagant. You know what artists are, too—no morals at all."

Poirot did not pay much attention to Japp's sweeping strictures on the artistic temperament. Instead he smiled knowingly.

"My good Japp, is it possible that you throw the mud in my eyes? I know well enough that it is the Chinaman you suspect. But you are so artful. You want me to help you—and yet you drag the red kipper across the trail."

Japp burst out laughing.

"That's you all over, Mr. Poirot. Yes, I'd bet on the Chink, I'll admit it now. It stands to reason that it was he who doctored the curry, and if he'd try once in an evening to get his master out of the way, he'd try twice."

"I wonder if he would," said Poirot softly.

"But it's the motive that beats me. Some heathen revenge or other, I suppose."

"I wonder," said Poirot again. "There has been no robbery? Nothing has disappeared? No jewellery, or money, or papers?"

"No—that is, not exactly."

I pricked up my ears; so did Poirot.

"There's been no robbery, I mean," explained Japp. "But the old boy was writing a book of some sort. We only knew about it this morning when there was a letter from the publishers asking about the manuscript. It was just completed, it seems. Young Paynter and I have searched high and low, but can't find a trace of it—he must have hidden it away somewhere."

Poirot's eyes were shining with the green light I knew so well.

"How was it called, this book?" he asked.

"*The Hidden Hand in China,* I think it was called."

"Aha!" said Poirot, with almost a gasp. Then he said quickly, "Let me see the Chinaman, Ah Ling."

The Chinaman was sent for and appeared, shuffling

along, with his eyes cast down, and his pigtail swinging. His impassive face showed no trace of any kind of emotion.

"Ah Ling," said Poirot, "are you sorry your master is dead?"

"I welly sorry. He good master."

"You know who kill him?"

"I not know. I tell pleeceman if I know."

The questions and answers went on. With the same impassive face, Ah Ling described how he had made the curry. The cook had had nothing to do with it, he declared, no hand had touched it but his own. I wondered if he saw where his admission was leading him. He stuck to it too, that the window to the garden was bolted that evening. If it was open in the morning, his master must have opened it himself. At last Poirot dismissed him.

"That will do, Ah Ling." Just as the Chinaman had got to the door, Poirot recalled him. "And you know nothing, you say, of the Yellow Jasmine?"

"No, what should I know?"

"Nor yet of the sign that was written underneath it?"

Poirot leant forward as he spoke, and quickly traced something on the dust of a little table. I was near enough to see it before he rubbed it out. A downstroke, a line at right angles, and then a second line down which completed a big 4. The effect on the Chinaman was electrical. For one moment his face was a mask of terror. Then, as suddenly, it was impassive again, and repeating his grave disclaimer, he withdrew.

Japp departed in search of young Paynter, and Poirot and I were left alone together.

"The Big Four, Hastings," cried Poirot. "Once again, the Big Four. Paynter was a great traveller. In his book there was doubtless some vital information concerning the doings of Number One, Li Chang Yen, the head and brains of the Big Four."

"But who—how—"

"Hush, here they come."

Gerald Paynter was an amiable, rather weak-looking young man. He had a soft brown beard, and a peculiar flowing tie. He answered Poirot's questions readily enough.

"I dined out with some neighbours of ours, the Wycherlys," he explained. "What time did I get home? Oh, about eleven. I had a latch-key, you know. All the servants had gone to bed, and I naturally thought my uncle had done the same. As a matter of fact, I did think I caught sight of that soft-footed Chinese beggar Ah Ling just whisking round the corner of the hall, but I fancy I was mistaken."

"When did you last see your uncle, Mr. Paynter? I mean before you came to live with him."

"Oh! not since I was a kid of ten. He and his brother (my father) quarrelled, you know."

"But he found you again with very little trouble, did he not? In spite of all the years that had passed?"

"Yes, it was quite a bit of luck my seeing the lawyer's advertisement."

Poirot asked no more questions.

Our next move was to visit Dr. Quentin. His story was substantially the same as he had told at the inquest, and he had little to add to it. He received us in his surgery, having just come to the end of his consulting patients. He seemed an intelligent man. A certain primness of manner went well with his pince-nez, but I fancied that he would be thoroughly modern in his methods.

"I wish I could remember about the window," he said frankly. "But it's dangerous to think back, one becomes quite positive about something that never existed. That's psychology, isn't it, M. Poirot? You see, I've read all about your methods, and I may say I'm an enormous admirer of yours. No, I suppose it's pretty certain that the Chinaman put the powdered opium in the curry, but he'll never admit it, and we shall never know why. But holding a man down in a fire—that's not in keeping with our Chinese friend's character, it seems to me."

I commented on this last point to Poirot as we walked down the main street of Market Handford.

"Do you think he let a confederate in?" I asked. "By the way, I suppose Japp can be trusted to keep an eye on him?" (The Inspector had passed into the police station on some business or other.) "The emissaries of the Big Four are pretty spry."

"Japp is keeping an eye on both of them," said Poirot grimly. "They have been closely shadowed ever since the body was discovered."

"Well, at any rate *we* know that Gerald Paynter had nothing to do with it."

"You always know so much more than I do, Hastings, that it becomes quite fatiguing."

"You old fox," I laughed. "You never will commit yourself."

"To be honest, Hastings, the case is now quite clear to me—all but the words, *Yellow Jasmine*—and I am coming to agree with you that they have no bearing on the crime. In a case of this kind, you have got to make up your mind who is lying. I have done that. And yet—"

He suddenly darted from my side and entered an adjacent bookshop. He emerged a few minutes later, hugging a parcel. Then Japp rejoined us, and we all sought quarters at the inn.

I slept late the next morning. When I descended to the sitting-room reserved for us, I found Poirot already there, pacing up and down, his face contorted with agony.

"Do not converse with me," he cried, waving an agitated hand. "Not until I know that all is well—that the arrest is made. Ah! but my psychology has been weak. Hastings, if a man writes a dying message, it is because it is important. Every one has said—'Yellow Jasmine? There is yellow jasmine growing up the house—it means nothing.'"

"Well, what does it mean? Just what it says. Listen." He held up a little book he was holding.

"My friend, it struck me that it would be well to

inquire into the subject. What exactly is yellow jasmine? This little book has told me. Listen."

He read.

" '*Gelsemini Radix*. Yellow Jasmine. Composition: Alkaloids *gelseminine* $C_{22}H_{26}N_2O_3$, a potent poison acting like coniine; *gelsemine* $C_{12}H_{14}NO_2$, acting like strychnine; *gelsemic acid,* etc. Gelsemium is a powerful depressant to the central nervous system. At a late stage in its action it paralyses the motor nerve endings, and in large doses causes giddiness and loss of muscular power. Death is due to paralysis of the respiratory centre.'

"You see, Hastings? At the beginning I had an inkling of the truth when Japp made his remark about a live man being forced into the fire. I realised then that it was a dead man who was burned."

"But why? What was the point?"

"My friend, if you were to shoot a man, or stab a man after he were dead, or even knock him on the head, it would be apparent that the injuries were inflicted after death. But with his head charred to a cinder, no one is going to hunt about for obscure causes of death, and a man who has apparently just escaped being poisoned at dinner, is not likely to be poisoned just afterwards. *Who* is lying, that is always the question. I decided to believe Ah Ling—"

"What!" I exclaimed.

"You are surprised, Hastings? Ah Ling knew of the existence of the Big Four, that was evident—so evident that it was clear he knew nothing of their association with the crime until that moment. Had he been the murderer, he would have been able to retain his impassive face perfectly. So I decided then, to believe Ah Ling, and I fixed my suspicions on Gerald Paynter. It seemed to me that Number Four would have found an impersonation of a long lost nephew very easy."

"What!" I cried. "Number Four?"

"No, Hastings, *not* Number Four. As soon as I had read

up the subject of yellow jasmine, I saw the truth. In fact, it leapt to the eye."

"As always," I said coldly, "it doesn't leap to mine."

"Because you will not use your little gray cells. Who had a chance to tamper with the curry?"

"Ah Ling. No one else."

"No one else? *What about the doctor?*"

"But that was *afterwards.*"

"Of course it was afterwards. There was no trace of powdered opium in the curry served to Mr. Paynter, but acting in obedience to the suspicions Dr. Quentin had aroused, the old man eats none of it, and preserves it to give to his medical attendant, whom he summons according to plan. Dr. Quentin arrives, takes charge of the curry, *and gives Mr. Paynter an injection*—of strychnine, he says, but really of yellow jasmine—a poisonous dose. When the drug begins to take effect, he departs, after unlatching the window. Then, in the night, he returns by the window, finds the manuscript, and shoves Mr. Paynter into the fire. He does not heed the newspaper that drops to the floor and is covered by the old man's body. Paynter knew what drug he had been given, and strove to accuse the Big Four of his murder. It is easy for Quentin to mix powdered opium with the curry before handing it over to be analysed. He gives his version of the conversation with the old man, and mentions the strychnine injection casually, in case the mark of the hypodermic needle is noticed. Suspicion at once is divided between accident and the guilt of Ah Ling owing to the poison in the curry."

"But Dr. Quentin cannot be Number Four?"

"I fancy he can. There is undoubtedly a real Dr. Quentin who is probably abroad somewhere. Number Four has simply masqueraded as him for a short time. The arrangements with Dr. Bolitho were all carried out by correspondence, the man who was to do locum originally having been taken ill at the last minute."

At that minute, Japp burst in, very red in the face.

"You have got him?" cried Poirot anxiously.

Japp shook his head, very out of breath.

"Bolitho came back from his holiday this morning—recalled by telegram. No one knows who sent it. The other man left last night. We'll catch him yet, though."

Poirot shook his head quietly.

"I think not," he said, and absent-mindedly he drew a big 4 on the table with a fork.

Chapter XI

A Chess Problem

POIROT and I often dined at a small restaurant in Soho. We were there one evening, when we observed a friend at an adjacent table. It was Inspector Japp, and as there was room at our table, he came and joined us. It was some time since either of us had seen him.

"Never do you drop in to see us nowadays," declared Poirot reproachfully. "Not since the affair of the Yellow Jasmine have we met, and that is nearly a month ago."

"I've been up north—that's why. How are things with you? Big Four still going strong—eh?"

Poirot shook a finger at him reproachfully.

"Ah! you mock yourself at me—but the Big Four—they exist."

"Oh! I don't doubt that—but they're not the hub of the universe, as you make out."

"My friend, you are very much mistaken. The greatest power for evil in the world to-day is this 'Big Four.' To what end they are tending, no one knows, but there has never been another such criminal organisation. The finest brain in China at the head of it, an American millionaire, and a French woman scientist as members, and for the fourth—"

Japp interrupted.

"I know—I know. Regular bee in your bonnet over it all. It's becoming your little mania, Moosior Poirot. Let's talk of something else for a change. Take any interest in chess?"

"I have played it, yes."

"Did you see that curious business yesterday? Match between two players of world-wide reputation, and one died during the game?"

"I saw a mention of it. Dr. Savaronoff, the Russian champion, was one of the players, and the other, who succumbed to heart failure, was the brilliant young American, Gilmour Wilson."

"Quite right. Savaronoff beat Rubinstein and became Russian champion some years ago. Wilson is said to be a second Capablanca."

"A very curious occurrence," mused Poirot. "If I mistake not, you have a particular interest in the matter?"

Japp gave a rather embarrassed laugh.

"You've hit it, Moosior Poirot. I'm puzzled. Wilson was sound as a bell—no trace of heart trouble. His death is quite inexplicable."

"You suspect Dr. Savaronoff of putting him out of the way?" I cried.

"Hardly that," said Japp dryly. "I don't think even a Russian would murder another man in order not to be beaten at chess—and anyway, from all I can make out, the boot was likely to be on the other leg. The doctor is supposed to be very hot stuff—second to Lasker they say he is."

Poirot nodded thoughtfully.

"Then what exactly is your little idea?" he asked. "Why should Wilson be poisoned? For, I assume, of course, that it is poison you suspect."

"Naturally. Heart failure means your heart stops beating—that's all there is to that. That's what a doctor says officially at the moment, but privately he tips us the wink that he's not satisfied."

"When is the autopsy to take place?"

"To-night. Wilson's death was extraordinarily sudden.

He seemed quite as usual and was actually moving one of the pieces when he suddenly fell forward—dead!"

"There are very few poisons that would act in such a fashion," objected Poirot.

"I know. The autopsy will help us, I expect. But why should anyone want Gilmour Wilson out of the way—that's what I'd like to know? Harmless unassuming young fellow. Just come over here from the States, and apparently hadn't an enemy in the world."

"It seems incredible," I mused.

"Not at all," said Poirot, smiling. "Japp has his theory, I can see."

"I have, Moosior Poirot. I don't believe the poison was meant for Wilson—it was meant for the other man."

"Savaronoff?"

"Yes. Savaronoff fell foul of the Bolsheviks at the outbreak of the Revolution. He was even reported killed. In reality he escaped, and for three years endured incredible hardships in the wilds of Siberia. His sufferings were so great that he is now a changed man. His friends and acquaintances declare they would hardly have recognised him. His hair is white, and his whole aspect that of a man terribly aged. He is a semi-invalid, and seldom goes out, living alone with a niece, Sonia Daviloff, and a Russian man-servant in a flat down Westminster way. It is possible that he still considers himself a marked man. Certainly he was very unwilling to agree to this chess contest. He refused several times point blank, and it was only when the newspapers took it up and began making a fuss about the 'unsportsman-like refusal' that he gave in. Gilmour Wilson had gone on challenging him with real Yankee pertinacity, and in the end he got his way. Now I ask you, Moosior Poirot, why wasn't he willing? Because he didn't want attention drawn to him. Didn't want somebody or other to get on his track. That's my solution—Gilmour Wilson got pipped by mistake."

"There is no one who has any private reason to gain by Savaronoff's death?"

"Well, his niece, I suppose. He's recently come into an immense fortune. Left him by Madame Gospoja whose husband was a sugar profiteer under the old regime. They had an affair together once, I believe, and she refused steadfastly to credit the reports of his death."

"Where did the match take place?"

"In Savaronoff's own flat. He's an invalid, as I told you."

"Many people there to watch it?"

"At least a dozen—probably more."

Poirot made an expressive grimace.

"My poor Japp, your task is not an easy one."

"Once I know definitely that Wilson was poisoned, I can get on."

"Has it occurred to you that, in the meantime, supposing your assumption that Savaronoff was the intended victim to be correct, the murderer may try again?"

"Of course it has. Two men are watching Savaronoff's flat."

"That will be very useful if any one should call with a bomb under his arm," said Poirot dryly.

"You're getting interested, Moosier Poirot," said Japp, with a twinkle. "Care to come round to the mortuary and see Wilson's body before the doctors start on it? Who knows, his tie-pin may be askew, and that may give you a valuable clue that will solve the mystery."

"My dear Japp, all through dinner my fingers have been itching to rearrange your own tie-pin. You permit, yes? Ah! that is much more pleasing to the eye. Yes, by all means, let us go to the mortuary."

I could see that Poirot's attention was completely captivated by this new problem. It was so long since he had shown any interest over any outside case that I was quite rejoiced to see him back in his old form.

For my own part, I felt a deep pity as I looked down upon the motionless form and convulsed face of the hapless young American who had come by his death in such a strange way. Poirot examined the body attentively. There was no mark on it anywhere, except a small scar on the left hand.

"And the doctor says that's a burn, not a cut," explained Japp.

Poirot's attention shifted to the contents of the dead man's pockets which a constable spread out for our inspection. There was nothing much—a handkerchief, keys, notecase filled with notes, and some unimportant letters. But one object standing by itself filled Poirot with interest.

"A chessman!" he exclaimed. "A white bishop. Was that in his pocket?"

"No, clasped in his hand. We had quite a difficulty to get it out of his fingers. It must be returned to Dr. Savaronoff sometime. It's part of a very beautiful set of carved ivory chessmen."

"Permit me to return it to him. It will make an excuse for my going there."

"Aha!" cried Japp. "So you want to come in on this ca⸮e?"

"I admit it. So skilfully have you aroused my interest."

"That's fine. Got you away from your brooding. Captain Hastings is pleased, too, I can see."

"Quite right," I said, laughing.

Poirot turned back towards the body.

"No other little detail you can tell me about—him?" he asked.

"I don't think so."

"Not even—that he was left-handed?"

"You're a wizard, Moosior Poirot. How did you know that? He *was* left-handed. Not that it's anything to do with the case."

"Nothing whatever," agreed Poirot hastily, seeing that Japp was slightly ruffled. "My little joke—that was all. I like to play you the trick, see you."

We went out upon an amicable understanding.

The following morning saw us wending our way to Dr. Savaronoff's flat in Westminster.

"Sonia Daviloff," I mused. "It's a pretty name."

Poirot stopped, and threw me a look of despair.

"Always looking for romance! You are incorrigible. It would serve you right if Sonia Daviloff turned out to be our friend and enemy the Countess Vera Rossakoff."

At the mention of the countess, my face clouded over.

"Surely, Poirot, you don't suspect—"

"But, no, no. It was a joke! I have not the Big Four on the brain to that extent, whatever Japp may say."

The door of the flat was opened to us by a man-servant with a peculiarly wooden face. It seemed impossible to believe that that impassive countenance could ever display emotion.

Poirot presented a card on which Japp had scribbled a few words of introduction, and we were shown into a low, long room furnished with rich hangings and curios. One or two wonderful ikons hung upon the walls, and exquisite Persian rugs lay upon the floor. A samovar stood upon a table.

I was examining one of the ikons which I judged to be of considerable value, and turned to see Poirot prone upon the floor. Beautiful as the rug was, it hardly seemed to me to necessitate such close attention.

"Is it such a very wonderful specimen?" I asked.

"Eh? Oh! the rug? But no, it was not the rug I was remarking. But it *is* a beautiful specimen, far too beautiful to have a large nail wantonly driven through the middle of it. No, Hastings," as I came forward, "the nail is not there now. But the hole remains."

A sudden sound behind us made me spin round, and Poirot spring nimbly to his feet. A girl was standing in the doorway. Her eyes, full upon us, were dark with suspicion. She was of medium height, with a beautiful, rather sullen face, dark blue eyes, and very black hair which was cut short. Her voice, when she spoke, was rich and sonorous, and completely un-English.

"I fear my uncle will be unable to see you. He is a great invalid."

"That is a pity, but perhaps you will kindly help me instead. You are Mademoiselle Daviloff, are you not?"

"Yes, I am Sonia Daviloff. What is it you want to know?"

"I am making some inquiries about that sad affair the night before last—the death of M. Gilmour Wilson. What can you tell me about it?"

The girl's eyes opened wide.

"He died of heart failure—as he was playing chess."

"The police are not so sure that it was—heart failure, mademoiselle."

The girl gave a terrified gesture.

"It was true then," she cried. "Ivan was right."

"Who is Ivan, and why do you say he was right?"

"It was Ivan who opened the door to you—and he has already said to me that in his opinion Gilmour Wilson did not die a natural death—that he was poisoned by mistake."

"By mistake."

"Yes, the poison was meant for my uncle."

She had quite forgotten her first distrust now, and was speaking eagerly.

"Why do you say that, mademoiselle? Who should wish to poison Dr. Savaronoff?"

She shook her head.

"I do not know. I am all in the dark. And my uncle, he will not trust me. It is natural, perhaps. You see, he hardly knows me. He saw me as a child, and not since till I came to live with him here in London. But this much I do know, he is in fear of something. We have many secret societies in Russia, and one day I overheard something which made me think it was of just such a society he went in fear. Tell me, monsieur"—she came a step nearer, and dropped her voice—"have you ever heard of a society called the 'Big Four'?"

Poirot jumped nearly out of his skin. His eyes positively bulged with astonishment.

"Why do you—what do you know of the Big Four, mademoiselle?"

"There is such an association, then! I overheard a

reference to them, and asked my uncle about it afterwards. Never have I seen a man so afraid. He turned all white and shaking. He was in fear of them, monsieur, in great fear, I am sure of it. And, by mistake, they killed the American, Wilson."

"The Big Four," murmured Poirot. "Always the Big Four! An astonishing coincidence, mademoiselle; your uncle is still in danger. I must save him. Now recount to me exactly the events of that fatal evening. Show me the chessboard, the table, how the two men sat—everything."

She went to the side of the room and brought out a small table. The top of it was exquisite, inlaid with squares of silver and black to represent a chess-board.

"This was sent to my uncle a few weeks ago as a present, with the request that he would use it in the next match he played. It was in the middle of the room—so."

Poirot examined the table with what seemed to me quite unnecessary attention. He was not conducting the inquiry at all as I would have done. Many of his questions seemed to me pointless, and upon really vital matters he seemed to have no questions to ask. I concluded that the unexpected mention of the Big Four had thrown him completely off his balance.

After a minute examination of the table and the exact position it had occupied, he asked to see the chessmen. Sonia Daviloff brought them to him in a box. He examined one or two of them in a perfunctory manner.

"An exquisite set," he murmured absent-mindedly.

Still not a question as to what refreshments there had been, or what people had been present.

I cleared my throat significantly.

"Don't you think, Poirot, that—"

He interrupted me peremptorily.

"Do not think, my friend. Leave all to me. Mademoiselle, is it quite impossible that I should see your uncle?"

A faint smile showed itself on her face.

"He will see you, yes. You understand, it is my part to interview all strangers first."

She disappeared. I heard a murmur of voices in the next room, and a minute later she came back and motioned us to pass into the adjoining room.

The man who lay there on a couch was an imposing figure. Tall, gaunt, with huge bushy eyebrows and white beard, and a face haggard as the result of starvation and hardships, Dr. Savaronoff was a distinct personality. I noted the peculiar formation of his head, its unusual height. A great chess player must have a great brain, I knew. I could easily understand Dr. Savaronoff being the second greatest player in the world.

Poirot bowed.

"M. le Docteur, may I speak to you alone?"

Savaronoff turned to his niece.

"Leave us, Sonia."

She disappeared obediently.

"Now, sir, what is it?"

"Dr. Savaronoff, you have recently come into an enormous fortune. If you should—die unexpectedly, who inherits it?"

"I have made a will leaving everything to my niece, Sonia Daviloff. You do not suggest—"

"I suggest nothing, but you have not seen your niece since she was a child. It would have been easy for any one to impersonate her."

Savaronoff seemed thunderstruck by the suggestion. Poirot went on easily.

"Enough as to that. I give you the word of warning, that is all. What I want you to do now is to describe to me the game of chess the other evening."

"How do you mean—describe it?"

"Well, I do not play the chess myself, but I understand that there are various regular ways of beginning—the gambit, do they not call it?"

Dr. Savaronoff smiled a little.

"Ah! I comprehend you now. Wilson opened Ruy Lopez—one of the soundest openings there is, and one frequently adopted in tournaments and matches."

"And how long had you been playing when the tragedy happened?"

"It must have been about the third or fourth move when Wilson suddenly fell foward over the table, stone dead."

Poirot rose to depart. He flung out his last question as though it was of absolutely no importance, but I knew better.

"Had he had anything to eat or drink?"

"A whisky and soda, I think."

"Thank you, Dr. Savaronoff. I will disturb you no longer."

Ivan was in the hall to show us out. Poirot lingered on the threshold.

"The flat below this, do you know who lives there?"

"Sir Charles Kingwell, a member of Parliament, sir. It has been let furnished lately, though."

"Thank you."

We went out into the bright winter sunlight.

"Well, really, Poirot," I burst out. "I don't think you've distinguished yourself this time. Surely your questions were very inadequate."

"You think so, Hastings?" Poirot looked at me appealingly. "I was *boulversé,* yes. What would you have asked?"

I considered the question carefully, and then outlined my scheme to Poirot. He listened with what seemed to be close interest. My monologue lasted until we had nearly reached home.

"Very excellent, very searching, Hastings," said Poirot, as he inserted his key in the door and preceded me up the stairs. "But quite unnecessary."

"Unnecessary!" I cried, amazed. "If the man was poisoned—"

"Aha," cried Poirot, pouncing upon a note which lay on the table. "From Japp. Just as I thought." He flung it over to me. It was brief and to the point. No traces of poison had been found, and there was nothing to show how the man came by his death.

"You see," said Poirot, "our questions would have been quite unnecessary."

"You guessed this beforehand?"

" 'Forecast the probable result of the deal,' " quoted Poirot from a recent Bridge problem on which I had spent much time. "*Mon ami*, when you do that successfully, you do not call it guessing."

"Don't let's split hairs," I said impatiently. "You foresaw this?"

"I did."

"Why?"

Poirot put his hand into his pocket and pulled out—a white bishop.

"Why," I cried, "you forgot to give it back to Dr. Savaronoff."

"You are in error, my friend. That bishop still reposes in my left-hand pocket. I took its fellow from the box of chessmen Mademoiselle Daviloff kindly permitted me to examine. The plural of one bishop is two bishops."

He sounded the final "s" with a great hiss. I was completely mystified.

"But why did you take it?"

"*Parbleu*, I wanted to see if they were exactly alike."

He stood them on the table side by side.

"Well, they are, of course," I said, "exactly alike."

Poirot looked at them with his head on one side.

"They seem so, I admit. But one should take no fact for granted until it is proved. Bring me, I pray you, my little scales."

With infinite care he weighed the two chessmen, then turned to me with a face alight with triumph.

"I was right. See you, I was right. Impossible to deceive Hercule Poirot!"

He rushed to the telephone—waited impatiently.

"Is that Japp? Ah! Japp, it is you. Hercule Poirot

speaks. Watch the man-servant, Ivan. On no account let him slip through your fingers. Yes, yes, it is as I say."

He dashed down the receiver and turned to me.

"You see it not, Hastings? I will explain. Wilson was not poisoned, he was electrocuted. A thin metal rod passes up the middle of one of those chessmen. The table was prepared beforehand and set upon a certain spot on the floor. When the bishop was placed upon one of the silver squares, the current passed through Wilson's body, killing him instantly. The only mark was the electric burn upon his hand—his left hand, because he was left-handed. The 'special table' was an extremely cunning piece of mechanism. The table I examined was a duplicate, perfectly innocent. It was substituted for the other immediately after the murder. The thing was worked from the flat below, which, if you remember, was let furnished. But one accomplice at least was in Savaronoff's flat. The girl is an agent of the Big Four, working to inherit Savaronoff's money."

"And Ivan?"

"I strongly suspect that Ivan is none other than the famous Number Four."

"What?"

"Yes. The man is a marvellous character actor. He can assume any part he pleases."

I thought back over past adventures, the lunatic asylum keeper, the butcher's young man, the suave doctor, all the same man, and all totally unlike each other.

"It's amazing," I said at last. "Everything fits in. Savaronoff had an inkling of the plot, and that's why he was so averse to playing the match."

Poirot looked at me without speaking. Then he turned abruptly away, and began pacing up and down.

"Have you a book on chess by any chance, *mon ami?*" he asked suddenly.

"I believe I have somewhere."

It took me some time to ferret it out, but I found it at last, and brought it to Poirot, who sank down in a chair and started reading it with the greatest attention.

In about a quarter of an hour the telephone rang. I answered it. It was Japp. Ivan had left the flat, carrying a large bundle. He had sprung into a waiting taxi, and the chase had begun. He was evidently trying to lose his pursuers. In the end he seemed to fancy that he had done so, and had then driven to a big empty house at Hampstead. The house was surrounded.

I recounted all this to Poirot. He merely stared at me as though he scarcely took in what I was saying. He held out the chess book.

"Listen to this, my friend. This is the Ruy Lopez opening. 1 P-K4, P-K4; 2 Kt-KB3, Kt-QB3; 3B-Kt5. Then there comes a question as to Black's best third move. He has the choice of various defences. It was White's third move that killed Gilmour Wilson, 3B-Kt5. Only the third move—does that say nothing to you?"

I hadn't the least idea what he meant, and told him so.

"Suppose, Hastings, that while you were sitting in this chair, you heard the front door being opened and shut, what would you think?"

"I should think some one had gone out, I suppose."

"Yes—but there are always two ways of looking at things. Some one gone out—some one come *in*—two totally different things, Hastings. But if you assumed the wrong one, presently some little discrepancy would creep in and show you that you were on the wrong track."

"What does all this mean, Poirot?"

Poirot sprang to his feet with sudden energy.

"It means that I have been a triple imbecile. Quick, quick, to the flat in Westminster. We may yet be in time."

We tore off in a taxi. Poirot returned no answer to my excited questions. We raced up the stairs. Repeated rings and knocks brought no reply, but listening closely I could distinguish a hollow groan coming from within.

The hall porter proved to have a master key, and after a few difficulties he consented to use it.

Poirot went straight to the inner room. A whiff of chloroform met us. On the floor was Sonia Daviloff, gagged and bound, with a great wad of saturated cotton wool over her nose and mouth. Poirot tore it off and began to take measures to restore her. Presently a doctor arrived, and Poirot handed her over to his charge and drew aside with me. There was no sign of Dr. Savaronoff.

"What does it all mean?" I asked, bewildered.

"It means that before two equal deductions I chose the wrong one. You heard me say that it would be easy for any one to impersonate Sonia Daviloff because her uncle had not seen her for so many years?"

"Yes?"

"Well, precisely the opposite held good also. It was equally easy for any one to impersonate the uncle."

"What?"

"Savaronoff *did* die at the outbreak of the Revolution. The man who pretended to have escaped with such terrible hardships, the man so changed 'that his own friends could hardly recognise him,' the man who successfully laid claim to an enormous fortune—"

"Yes. Who was he?"

"*Number Four.* No wonder he was frightened when Sonia let him know she had overheard one of his private conversations about the 'Big Four.' Again he has slipped through my fingers. He guessed I should get on the right track in the end, so he sent off the honest Ivan on a tortuous wild goose chase, chloroformed the girl, and got out, having by now doubtless realised most of the securities left by Madame Gospoja."

"But—but who tried to kill him then?"

"Nobody tried to kill *him*. Wilson was the intended victim all along."

"But why?"

"My friend, Savaronoff was the second greatest chess player in the world. In all probability Number Four did not even know the rudiments of the game. Certainly he could not sustain the fiction of a match. He tried all he knew to avoid the contest. When that failed, Wilson's doom was sealed. At all costs he must be prevented from discovering that the great Savaronoff did not even know how to play chess. Wilson was fond of the Ruy Lopez opening, and was certain to use it. Number Four arranged for death to come with the third move, before any complications of defence set in."

"But, my dear Poirot," I persisted, "are we dealing with a lunatic? I quite follow your reasoning, and admit that you must be right, but to kill a man just to sustain his role! Surely there were simpler ways out of the difficulty than that? He could have said that his doctor forbade the strain of a match."

Poirot wrinkled his forehead.

"*Certainement,* Hastings," he said, "there were other ways, but none so convincing. Besides, you are assuming that to kill a man is a thing to avoid, are you not? Number Four's mind, it does not act that way. I put myself in his place, a thing impossible for you. I picture his thoughts. He enjoys himself as the professor at that match. I doubt not he has visited the chess tourneys to study his part. He sits and frowns in thought; he gives the impression that he is thinking great plans, and all the time he laughs in himself. He is aware that two moves are all that he knows—and all that he *need know*. Again, it would appeal to his mind to foresee the events and to make the man his own executioner at the exact time that suits Number Four. . . . Oh, yes, Hastings, I begin to understand our friend and his psychology."

I shrugged.

"Well, I suppose you're right, but I can't understand any one running a risk he could so easily avoid."

"Risk!" Poirot snorted. "Where then lay the risk? Would Japp have solved the problem? No; if Number Four had not made one small mistake he would have run no risk."

"And his mistake?" I asked, although I suspected the answer.

"*Mon ami,* he overlooked the little gray cells of Hercule Poirot."

Poirot has his virtues, but modesty is not one of them.

Chapter XII

The Baited Trap

IT was mid-January—a typical English winter day in London, damp and dirty. Poirot and I were sitting in two chairs well drawn up to the fire. I was aware of my friend looking at me with a quizzical smile, the meaning of which I could not fathom.

"A penny for your thoughts," I said lightly.

"I was thinking, my friend, that at midsummer, when you first arrived, you told me that you proposed to be in this country for a couple of months only."

"Did I say that?" I asked, rather awkwardly. "I don't remember."

Poirot's smile broadened.

"You did, *mon ami*. Since then, you have changed your plan, is it not so?"

"Er—yes, I have."

"And why is that?"

"Dash it all, Poirot, you don't think I'm going to leave you all alone when you're up against a thing like the 'Big Four,' do you?"

Poirot nodded gently.

"Just as I thought. You are a staunch friend, Hastings. It is to serve me that you remain on here. And your wife—little Cinderella as you call her, what does she say?"

"I haven't gone into details, of course, but she understands. She'd be the last one to wish me to turn my back on a pal."

"Yes, yes, she, too, is a loyal friend. But it is going to be a long business, perhaps."

I nodded, rather discouraged.

"Six months already," I mused, "and where are we? You know, Poirot, I can't help thinking that we ought to—well, to do something."

"Always so energetic, Hastings! And what precisely would you have me do?"

This was somewhat of a poser, but I was not going to withdraw from my position.

"We ought to take the offensive," I urged. "What have we done all this time?"

"More than you think, my friend. After all, we have established the identity of Number Two and Number Three, and we have learnt more than a little about the ways and methods of Number Four."

I brightened up a little. As Poirot put it, things didn't sound so bad.

"Oh! Yes, Hastings, we have done a great deal. It is true that I am not in a position to accuse either Ryland or Madame Olivier—who would believe me? You remember I thought once I had Ryland successfully cornered? Nevertheless I have made my suspicions known in certain quarters—the highest—Lord Aldington, who enlisted my help in the matter of the stolen submarine plans, is fully cognisant of all my information respecting the Big Four—and while others may doubt, he believes. Ryland and Madame Olivier, and Li Chang Yen himself may go their ways, but there is a searchlight turned on all their movements."

"And Number Four?" I asked.

"As I said just now—I am beginning to know and understand his methods. You may smile, Hastings—but to penetrate a man's personality, to know exactly what he will do under any given circumstances—that is the beginning of success. It is a duel between us, and whilst he is constantly giving away his mentality to me, I endeavour to let him know little or nothing of mine. He is in the light, I in the shade. I tell you, Hastings, that every day they fear me the more for my chosen inactivity."

"They've let us alone, anyway," I observed. "There have been no more attempts on your life, and no ambushes of any kind."

"No," said Poirot thoughtfully. "On the whole, that rather surprises me. Especially as there are one or two fairly obvious ways of getting at us which I should have thought certain to have occurred to them. You catch my meaning, perhaps?"

"An infernal machine of some kind?" I hazarded.

Poirot made a sharp click with his tongue expressive of impatience.

"But no! I appeal to your imagination, and you can suggest nothing more subtle than bombs in the fireplace. Well, well, I have need of some matches, I will promenade myself despite the weather. Pardon, my friend, but is it possible that you read *The Future of the Argentine, Mirror of Society, Cattle Breeding, The Clue of Crimson* and *Sport in the Rockies* at one and the same time?"

I laughed, and admitted that *The Clue of Crimson* was at present engaging my sole attention. Poirot shook his head sadly.

"But replace then the others on the bookshelf! Never, never shall I see you embrace the order and the method. Mon Dieu, what then is a bookshelf for?"

I apologised humbly, and Poirot, after replacing the offending volumes, each in its appointed place, went out and left me to uninterrupted enjoyment of my selected book.

I must admit, however, that I was half asleep when Mrs. Pearson's knock at the door aroused me.

"A telegram for you, captain."

I tore the orange envelope open without much interest. Then I sat as though turned to stone.

It was a cable from Bronsen, my manager out at the South American ranch, and it ran as follows:—

"Mrs. Hastings disappeared yesterday, feared been kidnapped by some gang calling itself big four cable instructions have notified police but no clue as yet."

"BRONSEN."

I waved Mrs. Pearson out of the room, and sat as though stunned, reading the words over and over again. Cinderella—kidnapped! In the hands of the infamous Big Four! God, what could I do?

Poirot! I must have Poirot. He would advise me. He would checkmate them somehow. In a few minutes now, he would be back. I must wait patiently until then. But Cinderella—in the hands of the Big Four!

Another knock. Mrs. Pearson put her head in once more.

"A note for you, captain—brought by a heathen Chinaman. He's a-waiting downstairs."

I seized it from her. It was brief and to the point.

"If you ever wish to see your wife again, go with the bearer of this note immediately. Leave no message for your friend or she will suffer."

It was signed with a big 4.

What ought I to have done? What would you who read have done in my place?

I had no time to think. I saw only one thing—Cinderella in the power of those devils. I must obey—I dare not risk a hair of her head. I must go with this Chinaman and follow whither he led. It was a trap, yes, and it meant certain capture and possible death, but it was baited with the person dearest to me in the whole world, and I dared not hesitate.

What irked me most was to leave no word for Poirot. Once set him on my track, and all might yet be well? Dare I risk it? Apparently I was under no supervision, but yet I hesitated. It would have been so easy for the Chinaman to come up and assure himself that I was keeping to the letter of the command. Why didn't he? His very abstention made me more suspicious. I had seen so much of the omnipotence of the Big Four that I credited them with almost super-human powers. For all I knew, even the little bedraggled servant girl might be one of their agents.

No, I dared not risk it. But one thing I could do, leave the telegram. He would know then that Cinderella had disappeared, and who was responsible for her disappearance.

All this passed through my head in less time than it takes to tell, and I had clapped my hat on my head and was descending the stairs to where my guide waited, in a little over a minute.

The bearer of the message was a tall impassive Chinaman, neatly but rather shabbily dressed. He bowed and spoke to me. His English was perfect, but he spoke with a slight sing-song intonation.

"You Captain Hastings?"

"Yes," I said.

"You give me note, please."

I had foreseen the request, and handed him over the scrap of paper without a word. But that was not all.

"You have telegram to-day, yes? Come along just now? From South America, yes?"

I realised anew the excellence of their espionage system—or it might have been a shrewd guess. Bronsen was bound to cable me. They would wait until the cable was delivered and would strike hard upon it.

No good could come of denying what was palpably true.

"Yes," I said. "I did get a telegram."

"You fetch him, yes? Fetch him now."

I ground my teeth, but what could I do? I ran upstairs

again. As I did so, I thought of confiding in Mrs. Pearson, at any rate as far as Cinderella's disappearance went. She was on the landing, but close behind her was the little maid servant, and I hesitated. If she *was* a spy—the words of the note danced before my eyes. " . . . she will suffer. . . ." I passed into the sitting-room without speaking.

I took up the telegram and was about to pass out again when an idea struck me. Could I not leave some sign which would mean nothing to my enemies but which Poirot himself would find significant. I hurried across to the bookcase and tumbled out four books on to the floor. No fear of Poirot's not seeing them. They would outrage his eyes immediately—and coming on top of his little lecture, surely he would find them unusual. Next I put a shovelful of coal on the fire and managed to spill four knobs into the grate. I had done all I could—pray Heaven Poirot would read the sign aright.

I hurried down again. The Chinaman took the telegram from me, read it, then placed it in his pocket and with a nod beckoned me to follow him.

It was a long weary march that he led me. Once we took a bus and once we went for some considerable way in a train, and always our route led us steadily eastward. We went through strange districts, the existence I had never dreamed of. We were down by the docks now, I knew, and I realised that I was being taken into the heart of Chinatown.

In spite of myself I shivered. Still my guide plodded on, turning and twisting through mean streets and byways, until at last he stopped at a dilapidated house and rapped four times upon the door.

It was opened immediately by another Chinaman who stood aside to let us pass in. The clanging to of the door behind me was the knell of my last hopes. I was indeed in the hands of the enemy.

I was now handed over to the second Chinaman. He led me down some rickety stairs and into a cellar which was filled with bales and casks and which exhaled a pungent odour, as of Eastern spices. I felt wrapped all round with the atmosphere of the East, tortuous, cunning, sinister—

Suddenly my guide rolled aside two of the casks, and I saw a low tunnel-like opening in the wall. He motioned me to go ahead. The tunnel was of some length, and it was just too low for me to stand upright. At last, however, it broadened out into a passage, and a few minutes later we stood in another cellar.

My Chinaman went forward, and rapped four times on one of the walls. A whole section of the wall swung out, leaving a narrow doorway. I passed through, and to my utter astonishment found myself in a kind of Arabian Nights' palace. A low, long subterranean chamber hung with rich oriental silks, brilliantly lighted and fragrant with perfumes and spices. There were five or six silk covered divans, and exquisite carpets of Chinese workmanship covered the ground. At the end of the room was a curtained recess. From behind these curtains came a voice.

"You have brought our honoured guest?"

"Excellency, he is here," replied my guide.

"Let our guest enter," was the answer.

At the same moment, the curtains were drawn aside by an unseen hand, and I was facing an immense cushioned divan on which sat a tall thin Oriental dressed in wonderfully embroidered robes, and clearly, by the length of his finger nails, a great man.

"Be seated, I pray you, Captain Hastings," he said, with a wave of his hand. "You acceded to my request to come immediately, I am glad to see."

"Who are you?" I asked. "Li Chang Yen?"

"Indeed no, I am but the humblest of the master's servants. I carry out his behests, that is all—as do other of his servants in other countries—in South America, for instance."

I advanced a step.

"Where is she? What have you done with her out there?"

"She is in a place of safety—where none will find her. As yet, she is unharmed. You observe that I say—*as yet!*"

Cold shivers ran down my spine as I confronted this smiling devil.

"What do you want?" I cried. "Money?"

"My dear Captain Hastings. We have no designs on your small savings, I can assure you. Not—pardon me—a very intelligent suggestion on your part. Your colleague would not have made it, I fancy."

"I suppose," I said heavily, "you wanted to get me into your toils. Well, you have succeeded. I have come here with my eyes open. Do what you like with me, and let her go. She knows nothing, and she can be no possible use to you. You've used her to get hold of me—you've got me all right, and that settles it."

The smiling Oriental caressed his smooth cheek, watching me obliquely out of his narrow eyes.

"You go too fast," he said purringly. "That does not quite—settle it. In fact, to 'get hold of you' as you express it, is not really our objective. But through you, we hope to get hold of your friend, M. Hercule Poirot."

"I'm afraid you won't do that," I said, with a short laugh.

"What I suggest is this," continued the other, his words running on as though he had not heard me.

"You will write M. Hercule Poirot a letter, such a letter as will induce him to hasten hither and join you."

"I shall do no such thing," I said angrily.

"The consequences of refusal will be disagreeable."

"Damn your consequences."

"The alternative might be death!"

A nasty shiver ran down my spine, but I endeavoured to put a bold face upon it.

"It's no good threatening me, and bullying me. Keep your threats for Chinese cowards."

"My threats are very real ones, Captain Hastings. I ask you again, will you write this letter?"

"I will not, and what's more, you daren't kill me. You'd have the police on your tracks in no time."

My interlocutor clapped his hands swiftly. Two Chinese attendants appeared as it were out of the blue, and pinioned me by both arms. Their master said something rapidly to them in Chinese, and they dragged me across the floor to a spot in one corner of the big chamber. One of them stooped, and suddenly, without the least warning, the flooring gave beneath my feet. But for the restraining hand of the other man I should have gone down the yawning gap beneath me. It was inky black, and I could hear the rushing of water.

"The river," said my questioner from his place on the divan. "Think well, Captain Hastings. If you refuse again, you go headlong to eternity, to meet your death in the dark waters below. For the last time, will you write that letter?"

I'm not braver than most men. I admit frankly that I was scared to death, and in a blue funk. That Chinese devil meant business, I was sure of that. It was good-bye to the good old world. In spite of myself, my voice wobbled a little as I answered.

"For the last time, no! To hell with your letter!"

Then involuntarily I closed my eyes and breathed a short prayer.

Chapter XIII

The Mouse Walks In

NOT often in a life-time does a man stand on the edge of eternity, but when I spoke those words in that East End cellar I was perfectly certain that they were my last words on earth. I braced myself for the shock of those black, rushing waters beneath, and experienced in advance the horror of that breath-choking fall.

But to my surprise a low laugh fell on my ears. I opened my eyes. Obeying a sign from the man on the divan, my two jailers brought me back to my old seat facing him.

"You are a brave man, Captain Hastings," he said. "We of the East appreciate bravery. I may say that I expected you to act as you have done. That brings us to the appointed second act of our little drama. Death for yourself you have faced—will you face death for another?"

"What do you mean?" I asked hoarsely, a horrible fear creeping over me.

"Surely you have not forgotten the lady who is in our power—the Rose of the Garden."

I stared at him in dumb agony.

"I think, Captain Hastings, that you will write that letter. See, I have a cable form here. The message I shall write on it depends on you, and means life or death for your wife."

The sweat broke out on my brow. My tormentor continued, smiling amiably, and speaking with perfect sang-froid:—

"There, captain, the pen is ready to your hand. You have only to write. If not—"

"If not?" I echoed.

"If not, that lady that you love dies—and dies slowly. My master, Li Chang Yen, amuses himself in his spare hours by devising new and ingenious methods of torture—"

"My God!" I cried. "You fiend! Not that—you wouldn't do that—"

"Shall I recount to you some of his devices?"

Without heeding my cry of protest, his speech flowed on—evenly, serenely—till with a cry of horror I clapped my hands to my ears.

"It is enough, I see. Take up the pen and write."

"You would not dare—"

"Your speech is foolishness, and you know it. Take up the pen and write."

"If I do?"

"Your wife goes free. The cable shall be despatched immediately."

"How do I know that you will keep faith with me?"

"I swear it to you on the sacred tombs of my ancestors. Moreover, judge for yourself—why should I wish to do her harm? Her detention will have answered its purpose."

"And—and Poirot?"

"We will keep him in safe custody until we have concluded our operations. Then we will let him go."

"Will you swear that also on the tombs of your ancestors?"

"I have sworn one oath to you. That should be sufficient."

My heart sank. I was betraying my friend—to what? For a moment I hesitated—then the terrible alternative rose like a nightmare before my eyes. Cinderella—in the hands of these Chinese devils, dying by slow torture—

A groan rose to my lips. I seized the pen. Perhaps by

careful wording of the letter, I could convey a warning, and Poirot would be enabled to avoid the trap. It was the only hope.

But even that hope was not to remain. The Chinaman's voice rose, suave and courteous.

"Permit me to dictate to you."

He paused, consulted a sheaf of notes that lay by his side, and then dictated as follows:—

"Dear Poirot, I think I'm on the track of Number Four. A Chinaman came this afternoon and lured me down here with a bogus message. Luckily I saw through his little game in time, and gave him the slip. Then I turned the tables on him, and managed to do a bit of shadowing on my own account— rather neatly too, I flatter myself. I'm getting a bright young lad to carry this to you. Give him a half a crown, will you? That's what I promised him if it was delivered safely. I'm watching the house, and daren't leave. I shall wait for you until six o'clock, and if you haven't come then, I'll have a try at getting into the house on my own. It's too good a chance to miss, and, of course, the boy mightn't find you. But if he does, get him to bring you down here right away. And cover up those precious moustaches of yours in case any one's watching out from the house and might recognise you.

"Yours in haste,
"A. H."

Every word that I wrote plunged me deeper in despair. The thing was diabolically clever. I realised how closely every detail of our life must be known. It was just such an epistle as I might have penned myself. The acknowledgment that the Chinaman who had called that afternoon had endeavoured to "lure me away" discounted any good I might have done by leaving my "sign" of four books. It *had* been a trap, and I had seen through it, that was what Poirot would think. The time, too, was cleverly planned. Poirot, on receiving the note, would have just time to rush off with his innocent-looking guide, and that he would do so, I knew. My determination to make my way into the house would bring him posthaste. He always displayed a ridiculous distrust of my capacities. He would be convinced that I was running into danger without being equal to the situation, and would rush down to take command of the situation.

But there was nothing to be done. I wrote as bidden. My captor took the note from me, read it, then nodded his head approvingly and handed it to one of the silent attendants who disappeared with it behind one of the silken hangings on the wall which masked a doorway.

With a smile the man opposite to me picked up a cable form and wrote. He handed it to me.

It read: "Release the white bird with all despatch."

I gave a sigh of relief.

"You will send it at once?" I urged.

He smiled, and shook his head.

"When M. Hercule Poirot is in my hands it shall be sent. Not until then."

"But you promised—"

"If this device fails, I may have need of our white bird—to persuade you to further efforts."

I grew white with anger.

"My God! If you—"

He waved a long slim yellow hand.

"Be reassured, I do not think it will fail. And the moment M. Poirot is in our hands, I will keep my oath."

"If you play me false—"

"I have sworn it by my honoured ancestors. Have no fear. Rest here awhile. My servants will see to your needs whilst I am absent."

I was left alone in this strange underground nest of

luxury. The second Chinese attendant had reappeared. One of them brought food and drink and offered it to me, but I waved them aside. I was sick—sick—at heart—

And then suddenly the master reappeared tall and stately in his silken robes. He directed operations. By his orders I was hustled back through the cellar and tunnel into the original house I had entered. There they took me into a ground floor room. The windows were shuttered, but one could see through the cracks into the street. An old ragged man was shuffling along the opposite side of the road, and when I saw him make a sign to the window, I understood that he was one of the gang on watch.

"It is well," said my Chinese friend. "Hercule Poirot has fallen into the trap. He approaches now—and alone except for the boy who guides him. Now, Captain Hastings, you have still one more part to play. Unless you show yourself he will not enter the house. When he arrives opposite, you must go out on the step and beckon him in."

"What?" I cried, revolted.

"You play that part alone. Remember the price of failure. If Hercule Poirot suspects anything is amiss and does not enter the house, your wife dies by the Seventy Lingering Deaths! Ah! Here he is."

With a beating heart, and a feeling of deathly sickness, I looked through the crack in the shutters. In the figure walking along the opposite side of the street I recognised my friend at once, though his coat collar was turned up and an immense yellow muffler hid the bottom part of his face. But there was no mistaking that walk, and the poise of that egg-shaped head.

It was Poirot, coming to my aid in all good faith, suspecting nothing amiss. By his side ran a typical London urchin, grimy of face and ragged of apparel.

Poirot paused, looking across at the house, whilst the boy spoke to him eagerly and pointed. It was the time for me to act. I went out in the hall. At a sign from the tall Chinaman, one of the servants unlatched the door.

"Remember the price of failure," said my enemy in a low voice.

I was outside on the steps. I beckoned to Poirot. He hastened across.

"Aha! So all is well with you, my friend. I was beginning to be anxious. You managed to get inside? Is the house empty, then?"

"Yes," I said, in a voice I strove to make natural. "There must be a secret way out of it somewhere. Come in and let us look for it."

I stepped back across the threshold. In all innocence Poirot prepared to follow me.

And then something seemed to snap in my head. I saw only too clearly the part I was playing—the part of Judas.

"Back, Poirot!" I cried. "Back for your life. It's a trap. Never mind me. Get away at once."

Even as I spoke—or rather shouted my warning hands gripped me like a vice. One of the Chinese servants sprang past me to grab Poirot.

I saw the latter spring back, his arm raised, then suddenly a dense volume of smoke was rising round me, choking me—killing me—

I felt myself falling—suffocating—this was death—

I came to myself slowly and painfully—all my senses dazed. The first thing I saw was Poirot's face. He was sitting opposite me watching me with an anxious face. He gave a cry of joy when he saw me looking at him.

"Ah, you revive—you return to yourself. All is well! My friend—my poor friend!"

"Where am I?" I said painfully.

"Where? But *chez vous!*"

I looked round me. True enough, I was in the old familiar surroundings. And in the grate were the identical four knobs of coal I had carefully spilt there.

Poirot had followed my glance.

"But yes, that was a famous idea of yours—that and

the books. See you, if they should say to me any time, 'That friend of yours, that Hastings, he has not the great brain, is it not so?' I shall reply to them: 'You are in error.' It was an idea magnificent and superb that occurred to you there."

"You understood their meaning then?"

"Am I an imbecile? Of course I understood. It gave me just the warning I needed, and the time to mature my plans. Somehow or other the Big Four had carried you off. With what object? Clearly not for your *beaux yeux*—equally clearly not because they feared you and wanted to get you out of the way. No, their object was plain. You would be used as a decoy to get the great Hercule Poirot into their clutches. I have long been prepared for something of the kind. I make my little preparations, and presently, sure enough, the messenger arrives—such an innocent little street urchin. Me, I swallow everything, and hasten away with him, and, very fortunately, they permit you to come out on the doorstep. That was my one fear, that I should have to dispose of them before I had reached the place where you were concealed, and that I should have to search for you—perhaps in vain—afterwards."

"Dispose of them, did you say?" I asked feebly. "Single-handed?"

"Oh, there is nothing very clever about that. If one is prepared in advance all is simple—the motto of the Boy Scout, is it not? And a very fine one. Me, I was prepared. Not so long ago, I rendered a service to a very famous chemist, who did a lot of work in connection with poison gas during the war. He devised for me a little bomb—simple and easy to carry about—one has but to throw it and poof, the smoke—and then the unconsciousness. Immediately I blow a little whistle and straightway some of Japp's clever fellows who were watching the house here long before the boy arrived, and who managed to follow us all the way to Limehouse, came flying up and took charge of the situation."

"But how was it you weren't unconscious too?"

"Another piece of luck. Our friend Number Four (who

certainly composed that ingenious letter) permitted himself a little jest at my moustaches, which rendered it extremely easy for me to adjust my respirator under the guise of a yellow muffler."

"I remember," I cried eagerly, and then with the word "remember" all the ghastly horror that I had temporarily forgotten came back to me. *Cinderella—*

I fell back with a groan.

I must have lost consciousness again for a minute or two. I awoke to find Poirot forcing some brandy between my lips.

"What is it, *mon ami*? But what is it—then? Tell me."

Word by word, I got the thing told, shuddering as I did so. Poirot uttered a cry.

"My friend! My friend! But what you must have suffered! And I who knew nothing of all this! But reassure yourself! All is well!"

"You will find her, you mean? But she is in South America. And by the time we get there—long before, she will be dead—and God knows how and in what horrible way she will have died."

"No, no, you do not understand. She is safe and well. She has never been in their hands for one instant."

"But I got a cable from Bronsen?"

"No, no, you did not. You may have got a cable from South America signed Bronsen—that is a very different matter. Tell me, has it never occurred to you that an organisation of this kind, with ramifications all over the world, might easily strike at us through that little girl, Cinderella, whom you love so well?"

"No, never," I replied.

"Well, it did to me. I said nothing to you because I did not want to upset you unnecessarily—but I took measures of my own. Your wife's letters all seem to have been written from the ranch, but in reality she has been in a place of safety devised by me for over three months."

I looked at him for a long time.

"You are sure of that?"

"Parbleu! I know it. They tortured you with a lie!"

I turned my head aside. Poirot put his hand on my shoulder. There was something in his voice that I had never heard there before.

"You like not that I should embrace you or display the emotion, I know well. I will be very British. I will say nothing—but nothing at all. Only this—that in this last adventure of ours, the honours are all with you, and happy is the man who has such a friend as I have!"

CHAPTER XIV

THE PEROXIDE BLONDE

I was very disappointed with the results of Poirot's bomb attack on the premises in Chinatown. To begin with, the leader of the gang had escaped. When Japp's men rushed up in response to Poirot's whistle they found four Chinamen unconscious in the hall, but the man who had threatened me with death was not among them. I remembered afterwards that when I was forced out on to the doorstep, to decoy Poirot into the house, this man had kept well in the background. Presumably he was out of the danger zone of the gas bomb, and made good his escape by one of the many exits which we afterwards discovered.

From the four who remained in our hands we learnt nothing. The fullest investigation by the police failed to bring to light anything to connect them with the Big Four. They were ordinary low-class residents of the district, and they professed bland ignorance of the name Li Chang Yen. A Chinese gentleman had hired them for service in the house by the waterside, and they knew nothing whatever of his private affairs.

By the next day I had, except for a slight headache, completely recovered from the effects of Poirot's gas bomb. We went down together to Chinatown and searched the house from which I had been rescued. The premises consisted of two ramshackle houses joined together by an underground passage. The ground floors and the upper stories of each were unfurnished and deserted, the broken windows covered by decaying shutters. Japp had already been prying about in the cellars, and had discovered the secret of the entrance to the subterranean chamber where I had spent such an unpleasant half-hour. Closer investigation confirmed the impression that it had made on me the night before. The silks on the walls and divan and the carpets on the floors were of exquisite workmanship. Although I know very little about Chinese art, I could appreciate that every article in the room was perfect of its kind.

With the aid of Japp and some of his men we conducted a most thorough search of the apartment. I had cherished high hopes that we would find documents of importance. A list, perhaps, of some of the more important agents of the Big Four, or cipher notes of some of their plans, but we discovered nothing of the kind. The only papers we found in the whole place were the notes which the Chinaman had consulted whilst he was dictating the letter to Poirot. These consisted of a very complete record of each of our careers, and estimate of our characters, and suggestions about the weaknesses through which we might best be attacked.

Poirot was most childishly delighted with this discovery. Personally I could not see that it was of any value whatever, especially as whoever compiled the notes was ludicrously mistaken in some of his opinions. I pointed this out to my friend when we were back in our rooms.

"My dear Poirot," I said, "you know now what the enemy thinks of us. He appears to have a grossly exaggerated idea of your brain power, and to have absurdly underrated mine, but I do not see how we are better off for knowing this."

Poirot chuckled in rather an offensive way.

"You do not see, Hastings, no? But surely now we can prepare ourselves for some of their methods of attack now that we are warned of some of our faults. For instance my friend, we know that you should think before you act.

Again, if you meet a red-haired young woman in trouble you should eye her—what you say—askance, is it not?"

Their notes had contained some absurd references to my supposed impulsiveness, and had suggested that I was susceptible to the charms of young women with hair of a certain shade. I thought Poirot's reference to be in the worst of taste, but fortunately I was able to counter him.

"And what about you?" I demanded. "Are you going to try to cure your 'overweening vanity?' Your 'finicky tidiness'?"

I was quoting, and I could see that he was not pleased with my retort.

"Oh, without doubt, Hastings, in some things they deceive themselves—*tant mieux!* They will learn in due time. Meanwhile we have learnt something, and to know is to be prepared."

This last was a favourite axiom of his lately; so much so that I had begun to hate the sound of it.

"We know something, Hastings," he continued. "Yes, we know something—and that is to the good—but we do not know nearly enough. We must know more."

"In what way?"

Poirot settled himself back in his chair, straightened a box of matches which I had thrown carelessly down on the table, and assumed an attitude that I knew only too well. I saw that he was prepared to hold forth at some length.

"See you, Hastings, we have to contend against four adversaries; that is, against four different personalities. With Number One we have never come into personal contact—we know him, as it were, only by the impress of his mind—and in passing, Hastings, I will tell you that I begin to understand that mind very well—a mind most subtle and Oriental—every scheme and plot that we have encountered has emanated from the brain of Li Chang Yen. Number Two and Number Three are so powerful, so high up, that they are for the present immune from our attacks. Nevertheless what is their safeguard is, by a perverse chance, our safeguard also. They are so much in the limelight that their movements must be carefully ordered. And so we come to the last member of the gang—we come to the man known as Number Four."

Poirot's voice altered a little, as it always did when speaking of this particular individual.

"Number Two and Number Three are able to succeed, to go on their way unscathed, owing to their notoriety and their assured position. Number Four succeeds for the opposite reason—he succeeds by the way of obscurity. Who is he? Nobody knows. What does he look like? Again nobody knows. How many times have we seen him, you and I? Five times, is it not? And could either of us say truthfully that we could be sure of recognising him again?"

I was forced to shake my head, as I ran back in my mind over those five different people who, incredible as it seemed, were one and the same man. The burly lunatic asylum keeper, the man in the buttoned-up overcoat in Paris, James, the footman, the quiet young medical man in the Yellow Jasmine case, and the Russian Professor. In no way did any two of these people resemble each other.

"No," I said hopelessly. "We've nothing to go by whatsoever."

Poirot smiled.

"Do not, I pray of you, give way to such enthusiastic despair. We know one or two things."

"What kind of things?" I asked sceptically.

"We know that he is a man of medium height, and of medium or fair colouring. If he were a tall man of swarthy complexion he could never have passed himself off as the fair stocky doctor. It is child's play, of course, to put on an additional inch or so for the part of James, or the Professor. In the same way he must have a short straight nose. Additions can be built on to a nose by skilful makeup, but a large nose cannot be successfully reduced at a moment's notice. Then again, he must be a fairly young man, certainly not over thirty-five. You see, we are getting somewhere. A man between thirty and thirty-five, of medium height and colouring, an adept in the art of makeup, and with very few or any teeth of his own."

"What?"

"Surely, Hastings. As the keeper, his teeth were broken and discoloured, in Paris they were even and white, as the doctor they protruded slightly, and as Savaronoff they had unusually long canines. Nothing alters the face so completely as a different set of teeth. You see where all this is leading us?"

"Not exactly," I said cautiously.

"A man carries his profession written in his face, they say."

"He's a criminal," I cried.

"He is an adept in the art of making up."

"It's the same thing."

"Rather a sweeping statement, Hastings, and one which would hardly be appreciated by the theatrical world. Do you not see that the man is, or has been, at one time or another, an actor?"

"An actor?"

"But certainly. He has the whole technique at his finger-tips. Now there are two classes of actors, the one who sinks himself in his part, and the one who manages to impress his personality upon it. It is from the latter class that actor managers usually spring. They seize a part and mould it to their own personality. The former class is quite likely to spend its days doing Mr. Lloyd George at different music halls, or impersonating old men with beards in repertory plays. It is among that former class that we must look for our Number Four. He is a supreme artist in the way he sinks himself in each part he plays."

I was growing interested.

"So you fancy you may be able to trace his identity through his connection with the stage?"

"Your reasoning is always brilliant, Hastings."

"It might have been better," I said coldly, "if the idea had come to you sooner. We have wasted a lot of time."

"You are in error, *mon ami.* No more time has been wasted than was unavoidable. For some months now my agents have been engaged on the task. Joseph Aarons is one of them. You remember him? They have compiled a list for me of men fulfilling the necessary qualifications—young men round about the age of thirty, of more or less nondescript appearance, and with a gift for playing character parts—men, moreover, who have definitely left the stage within the last three years."

"Well?" I said, deeply interested.

"The list was, necessarily, rather a long one. For some time now, we have been engaged on the task of elimination. And finally we have boiled the whole thing down to four names. Here they are, my friend."

He tossed me over a sheet of paper. I read its contents aloud.

"Ernest Luttrell. Son of a North Country parson. Always had a kink of some kind in his moral make-up. Was expelled from his public school. Went on the stage at the age of twenty-three. (There followed a list of parts he had played, with dates and places.) Addicted to drugs. Supposed to have gone to Australia four years ago. Cannot be traced after leaving England. Age 32, height 5 ft. 10½ in., clean-shaven, hair brown, nose straight, complexion fair, eyes gray.

"John St. Maur. Assumed name. Real name not known. Believed to be of cockney extraction. On stage since quite a child. Did music hall impersonations. Not been heard of for three years. Age, about 33, height 5 ft. 10 in., slim build, blue eyes, fair colouring.

"Austen Lee. Assumed name. Real name Austen Foly. Good family. Always had taste for acting and distinguished himself in that way at Oxford. Brilliant war record. Acted in—(The usual list followed. It included many repretory plays.) An enthusiast on criminology. Had bad nervous breakdown as the result of a motor accident three and a half years ago, and has not appeared on the stage since. No clue to his present whereabouts. Age 35, height 5 ft. 9½ in., complexion fair, eyes blue, hair brown.

"Claud Darrell. Supposed to be real name. Some mystery about his origin. Played at music halls, and also in repertory plays. Seems to have had no intimate friends. Was in China in 1919. Returned by way of America. Played a few parts in New York. Did not appear on the stage one night, and has never been heard of since. New York police say most mysterious disappearance. Age about 33, hair brown, fair complexion, gray eyes. Height 5 ft. 10½ in.

"Most interesting," I said, as I laid down the paper. "And so this is the result of the investigation of months? These four names. Which of them are you inclined to suspect?"

Poirot made an eloquent gesture.

"*Mon ami,* for the moment it is an open question. I would just point out to you that Claud Darrell has been in China and America—a fact not without significance, perhaps, but we must not allow ourselves to be unduly biased by that point. It may be a mere coincidence."

"And the next step?" I asked eagerly.

"Affairs are already in train. Every day cautiously worded advertisements will appear. Friends and relatives of one or the other will be asked to communicate with my solicitor at his office. Even to-day we might— Aha, the telephone! Probably it is, as usual, the wrong number, and they will regret to have troubled us, but it may be—yes, it may be—that something has arisen."

I crossed the room and picked up the receiver.

"Yes, yes. M. Poirot's rooms. Yes, Captain Hastings speaking. Oh, it's you, Mr. McNeil! (McNeil and Hodgson were Poirot's solicitors.) I'll tell him. Yes, we'll come round at once."

I replaced the receiver and turned to Poirot, my eyes dancing with excitement.

"I say, Poirot, there's a woman there. Friend of Claud

Darrell's. Miss Flossie Monro. McNeil wants you to come round."

"At the instant!" cried Poirot, disappearing into his bedroom, and reappearing with a hat.

A taxi soon took us to our destination, and we were ushered into Mr. McNeil's private office. Sitting in the arm-chair facing the solicitor was a somewhat lurid looking lady no longer in her first youth. Her hair was of an impossible yellow, and was prolific in curls over each ear, her eyelids were heavily blackened, and she had by no means forgotten the rouge and the lip salve.

"Ah, here is M. Poirot!" said Mr. McNeil. "M. Poirot, this is Miss—er—Monro, who has very kindly called to give us some information."

"Ah, but that is most kind!" cried Poirot.

He came forward with great empressement, and shook the lady warmly by the hand.

"Mademoiselle blooms like a flower in this dry-as-dust old office," he added, careless of the feelings of Mr. McNeil.

This outrageous flattery was not without effect. Miss Monro blushed and simpered.

"Oh, go on now, Mr. Poirot!" she exclaimed. "I know what you Frenchmen are like."

"Mademoiselle, we are not mute like Englishmen before beauty. Not that I am a Frenchman—I am a Belgian, you see."

"I've been to Ostend myself," said Miss Monro.

The whole affair, as Poirot would have said, was marching splendidly.

"And so you can tell us something about Mr. Claud Darrell?" continued Poirot.

"I knew Mr. Darrell very well at one time," explained the lady. "And I saw your advertisement, being out of a shop for the moment, and my time being my own, I said to myself: There, they want to know about poor old Claudie— lawyers, too—maybe it's a fortune looking for the rightful heir, I'd better go round at once."

Mr. McNeil rose.

"Well, Monsieur Poirot, shall I leave you for a little conversation with Miss Monro?"

"You are too amiable. But stay—a little idea presents itself to me. The hour of the *déjeuner* approaches. Mademoiselle will perhaps honour me by coming out to luncheon with me?"

Miss Monro's eyes glistened. It struck me that she was in exceedingly low water, and that the chance of a square meal was not to be despised.

A few minutes later saw us all in a taxi, bound for one of London's most expensive restaurants. Once arrived there, Poirot ordered a most delectable lunch, and then turned to his guest.

"And for wine, mademoiselle? What do you say to champagne?"

Miss Monro said nothing—or everything.

The meal started pleasantly. Poirot replenished the lady's glass with thoughtful assiduity, and gradually slid on to the topic nearest his heart.

"The poor Mr. Darrell. What a pity he is not with us."

"Yes, indeed," sighed Miss Monro. "Poor boy, I do wonder what's become of him."

"It is a long time since you have seen him, yes?"

"Oh, simply ages—not since the war. He was a funny boy, Claudie, very close about things, never told you a word about himself. But, of course, that all fits in if he's a missing heir. Is it a title, Mr. Poirot?"

"Alas, a mere heritage," said Poirot unblushingly. "But you see, it may be a question of identification. That is why it is necessary for us to find some one who knew him very well indeed. You knew him very well, did you not, mademoiselle?"

"I don't mind telling you, Mr. Poirot. You're a gentleman. You know how to order a lunch for a lady—which is more than some of these young whippersnappers do nowadays. Downright mean, I call it. As I was saying, you being a Frenchman won't be shocked. Ah, you Frenchmen! Naughty, naughty!" She wagged her finger at him in an excess of archness. "Well, there it was, me and Claudie, two young things—what else could you expect? And I've still a kindly feeling for him. Though, mind you, he didn't treat me well—no, he didn't—he didn't treat me well at all. Not as a lady should be treated. They're all the same when it comes to a question of money."

"No, no, mademoiselle, do not say that," protested Poirot, filling up her glass once more. "Could you now describe this Mr. Darrell to me?"

"He wasn't anything so very much to look at," said Flossie Monro dreamily. "Neither tall nor short, you know, but quite well set up. Spruce-looking. Eyes a sort of blue-gray. And more or less fair-haired, I suppose. But oh, what an artist! I never saw any one to touch him in the profession! He'd have made his name before now if it hadn't been for jealousy. Ah, Mr. Poirot, jealousy—you wouldn't believe it, you really wouldn't, what we artists have to suffer through jealousy. Why, I remember once at Manchester—"

We displayed what patience we could in listening to a long complicated story about a pantomime, and the infamous conduct of the principal boy. Then Poirot led her gently back to the subject of Claud Darrell.

"It is very interesting, all this that you are able to tell us, mademoiselle, about Mr. Darrell. Women are such wonderful observers—they see everything, they notice the little detail that escapes the mere man. I have seen a woman identify one man out of a dozen others—and why, do you think? She had observed that he had a trick of stroking his nose when he was agitated. Now would a man ever have thought of noticing a thing like that?"

"Did you ever!" cried Miss Monro. "I suppose we do notice things. I remember Claudie, now I come to think of it, always fiddling with his bread at table. He'd get a little piece between his fingers and then dab it round to pick up crumbs. I've seen him do it a hundred times. Why, I'd know him anywhere by that one trick of his."

"Is not that just what I say? The marvellous observation of a woman. And did you ever speak to him about this little habit of his, mademoiselle?"

"No, I didn't, Mr. Poirot. You know what men are! They don't like you to notice things—especially if it should seem you were telling them off about it. I never said a word—but many's the time I smiled to myself. Bless you, he never knew he was doing it even."

Poirot nodded gently. I noticed that his own hand was shaking a little as he stretched it out to his glass.

"Then there is always handwriting as a means of establishing identity," he remarked. "Without doubt you have preserved a letter written by Mr. Darrell?"

Flossie Monro shook her head regretfully.

"He was never one for writing. Never wrote me a line in his life."

"That is a pity," said Poirot.

"I tell you what, though," said Miss Monro suddenly. "I've got a photograph if that would be any good?"

"You have a photograph?"

Poirot almost sprang from his seat with excitement.

"It's quite an old one—eight years old at least."

"*Ça ne fait rien!* No matter how old and faded! Ah, *ma foi,* but what stupendous luck! You will permit me to inspect that photograph, mademoiselle?"

"Why, of course."

"Perhaps you will even permit me to have a copy made? It would not take long."

"Certainly if you like."

Miss Monro rose.

"Well, I must run away," she declared archly. "Very glad to have met you and your friend, Mr. Poirot."

"And the photograph? When may I have it?"

"I'll look it out to-night. I think I know where to lay my hand upon it. And I'll send it to you right away."

"A thousand thanks, mademoiselle. You are all that is of the most amiable. I hope that we shall soon be able to arrange another little lunch together."

"As soon as you like," said Miss Monro. "I'm willing."

"Let me see, I do not think that I have your address?"

With a grand air, Miss Monro drew a card from her hand-bag, and handed it to him. It was a somewhat dirty card, and the original address had been scratched out and another substituted in pencil.

Then, with a good many bows and gesticulations on Poirot's part, we bade farewell to the lady and got away.

"Do you really think this photograph so important?" I asked Poirot.

"Yes, *mon ami*. The camera does not lie. One can magnify a photograph, seize salient points that otherwise would remain unnoticed. And then there are a thousand details—such as the structure of the ears, which no one could ever describe to you in words. Oh, yes, it is a great chance, this which has come our way! That is why I propose to take precautions."

He went across to the telephone as he finished speaking, and gave a number which I knew to be that of a private detective agency which he sometimes employed. His instructions were clear and definite. Two men were to go to the address he gave, and, in general terms, were to watch over the safety of Miss Monro. They were to follow her wherever she went.

Poirot hung up the receiver and came back to me.

"Do you really think that necessary, Poirot?" I asked.

"It may be. There is no doubt that we are watched, you and I, and since that is so, they will soon know with whom we were lunching to-day. And it is possible that Number Four will scent danger."

About twenty minutes later the telephone bell rang. I answered it. A curt voice spoke into the phone.

"Is that Mr. Poirot? St. James Hospital speaking. A young woman was brought in ten minutes ago. Street accident. Miss Flossie Monro. She is asking very urgently for Mr. Poirot. But he must come at once. She can't possibly last long."

I repeated the words to Poirot. His face went white.

"Quick, Hastings. We must go like the wind."

A taxi took us to the hospital in less than ten minutes. We asked for Miss Monro, and were taken immediately to the accident ward. But a white-capped sister met us in the doorway.

Poirot read the news in her face.

"It is over, eh?"

"She died six minutes ago."

Poirot stood as though stunned.

The nurse, mistaking his emotion, began speaking gently.

"She did not suffer, and she was unconscious towards the last. She was run over by a motor, you know—and the driver of the car did not even stop. Wicked, isn't it? I hope some one took the number."

"The stars fight against us," said Poirot, in a low voice.

"You would like to see her?"

The nurse led the way, and we followed.

Poor Flossie Monro, with her rouge and her dyed hair. She lay there very peacefully, with a little smile on her lips.

"Yes," murmured Poirot. "The stars fight against us— but is it the stars?" He lifted his head as though struck by a sudden idea. "Is it the stars, Hastings? If it is not—if it is not. . . . Oh, I swear to you, my friend, standing here by this poor woman's body, that I will have no mercy when the time comes!"

"What do you mean?" I asked.

But Poirot had turned to the nurse and was eagerly demanding information. A list of the articles found in her hand-bag was finally obtained. Poirot gave a suppressed cry as he read it over.

"You see, Hastings, you see?"

"See what?"

"There is no mention of a latch-key. But she must have had a latch-key with her. No, she was run down in cold blood, and the first person who bent over her took the key from her bag. But we may yet be in time. He may not have been able to find at once what he sought."

Another taxi took us to the address Flossie Monro had given us, a squalid block of Mansions in an unsavoury neighbourhood. It was some time before we could gain admission to Miss Monro's flat, but we had at least the satisfaction of knowing that no one could leave it whilst we were on guard outside.

Eventually we got in. It was plain that some one had been before us. The contents of drawers and cupboards were strewn all over the floor. Locks had been forced, and small tables had even been overthrown, so violent had been the searcher's haste.

Poirot began to hunt through the debris. Suddenly he stood erect with a cry, holding out something. It was an old-fashioned photograph frame—empty.

He turned it slowly over. Affixed to the back was a small round label—a price label.

"It cost four shillings," I commented.

"*Mon Dieu!* Hastings, use your eyes. That is a new clean label. It was stuck there by the man who took out the photograph, the man who was here before us, but knew that we should come, and so left this for us—Claud Darrell—alias Number Four!"

CHAPTER XV

THE TERRIBLE CATASTROPHE

IT was after the tragic death of Miss Flossie Monro that I began to be aware of a change in Poirot. Up to now, his invincible confidence in himself had stood the test. But it seemed as though, at last, the long strain was beginning to tell. His manner was grave and brooding, and his nerves were on edge. In these days he was as jumpy as a cat. He avoided all discussion of the Big Four as far as possible, and seemed to throw himself into his ordinary work with almost his old ardour. Nevertheless, I knew that he was secretly active in the big matter. Extraordinary-looking Slavs were constantly calling to see him, and though he vouchsafed no explanation as to these mysterious activities, I realised that he was building some new defence or weapon of opposition with the help of these somewhat repulsive-looking foreigners. Once, purely by chance, I happened to see the entries in his pass-book—he had asked me to verify some small item—and I noticed the paying out of a huge sum—a huge sum even for Poirot who was coining money nowadays—to some Russian with apparently every letter of the alphabet in his name.

But he gave no clue as to the line on which he proposed to operate. Only over and over again he gave utterance to one phrase. "It is the greatest mistake to underestimate your adversary. Remember that, *mon ami.*" And I realised that that was the pitfall he was striving at all costs to avoid.

So matters went on until the end of March, and then one morning Poirot made a remark which startled me considerably.

"This morning, my friend, I should recommend the best suit. We go to call upon the Home Secretary."

"Indeed? That is very exciting. He has called you in to take up a case?"

"Not exactly. The interview is of my seeking. You may remember my saying that I once did him some small service? He is inclined to be foolishly enthusiastic over my capabilities in consequence, and I am about to trade on this attitude of his. As you know, the French Premier, M. Desjardeaux is over in London, and at my request the Home Secretary has arranged for him to be present at our little conference this morning."

The Right Honourable Sydney Crowther, His Majesty's Secretary of State for Home Affairs, was a well-known and popular figure. A man of some fifty years of age, with a quizzical expression and shrewd gray eyes, he received us with that delightful bonhomie of manner which was well known to be one of his principal assets.

Standing with his back to the fireplace was a tall thin man with a pointed black beard and a sensitive face.

"M. Desjardeaux," said Crowther, "allow me to introduce to you M. Hercule Poirot of whom you may, perhaps, already have heard."

The Frenchman bowed and shook hands.

"I have indeed heard of M. Hercule Poirot," he said pleasantly. "Who has not?"

"You are too amiable, monsieur," said Poirot, bowing, but his face flushed with pleasure.

"Any word for an old friend?" asked a quiet voice, and a man came forward from a corner by a tall bookcase.

It was our old acquaintance, Mr. Ingles.

Poirot shook him warmly by the hand.

"And now, M. Poirot," said Crowther. "We are at your service. I understood you to say that you had a communication of the utmost importance to make to us."

"That is so, monsieur. There is in the world today a vast organisation—an organisation of crime. It is controlled by four individuals, who are known and spoken of as the Big Four. Number One is a Chinaman, Li Chang Yen; Number Two is the American multi-millionaire, Abe Ryland; Number Three is a Frenchwoman; Number Four I have every reason to believe is an obscure English actor called Claud Darrell. These four are banded together to destroy the existing social order, and to replace it with an anarchy in which they would reign as dictators."

"Incredible," muttered the Frenchman. "Ryland, mixed up with a thing of that kind? Surely the idea is too fantastic."

"Listen, monsieur, whilst I recount to you some of the doings of this Big Four."

It was an enthralling narrative which Poirot unfolded. Familiar as I was with all the details, they thrilled me anew as I heard the bald recital of our adventures and escapes.

M. Desjardeaux looked mutely at Mr. Crowther as Poirot finished. The other answered the look.

"Yes, M. Desjardeaux, I think we must admit the existence of a 'Big Four.' Scotland Yard was inclined to jeer at first, but they have been forced to admit that M. Poirot was right in many of his claims. The only question is the extent of its aims. I cannot but feel that M. Poirot—er—exaggerates a little."

For answer Poirot set forth ten salient points. I have been asked not to give them to the public even now, and so I refrain from doing so, but they included the extraordinary disasters to submarines which occurred in a certain month, and also a series of aeroplane accidents and forced landings. According to Poirot, these were all the work of the Big Four, and bore witness to the fact that they were in possession of various scientific secrets unknown to the world at large.

This brought us straight to the question which I had been waiting for the French Premier to ask.

"You say that the third member of this organisation is a Frenchwoman. Have you any idea of her name?"

"It is a well-known name, monsieur. An honoured name. Number Three is no less than the famous Madame Olivier."

At the mention of the world-famous scientist, successor to the Curies, M. Desjardeaux positively bounded from his chair, his face purple with emotion.

"Madame Olivier! Impossible! Absurd! It is an insult what you say there!"

Poirot shook his head gently, but made no answer.

Desjardeaux looked at him in stupefaction for some moments. Then his face cleared, and he glanced at the Home Secretary and tapped his forehead significantly.

"M. Poirot is a great man," he observed. "But even the great man—sometimes he has his little mania, does he not? And seeks in high places for fancied conspiracies. It is well known. You agree with me, do you not, Mr. Crowther?"

The Home Secretary did not answer for some minutes. Then he spoke slowly and heavily.

"Upon my soul, I don't know," he said at last. "I have always had and still have the utmost belief in M. Poirot, but—well, this takes a bit of believing."

"This Li Chang Yen, too," continued M. Desjardeaux. "Who has ever heard of him?"

"I have," said the unexpected voice of Mr. Ingles.

The Frenchman stared at him, and he stared placidly back again, looking more like a Chinese idol than ever. "Mr. Ingles," explained the Home Secretary, "is the greatest authority we have on the interior of China."

"And you have heard of this Li Chang Yen?"

"Until M. Poirot here came to me, I imagined that I was the only man in England who had. Make no mistake, M. Desjardeaux, there is only one man in China who counts to-day—Li Chang Yen. He has, perhaps, I only say perhaps, the finest brain in the world at the present time."

M. Desjardeaux sat as though stunned. Presently, however, he rallied.

"There may be something in what you say, M. Poirot," he said coldly. "But as regards Madame Olivier, you are most certainly mistaken. She is a true daughter of France, and devoted solely to the cause of science."

Poirot shrugged his shoulders and did not answer.

There was a minute or two's pause, and then my little friend rose to his feet, with an air of dignity that sat rather oddly upon his quaint personality.

"That is all I have to say, messieurs—to warn you. I thought it likely that I should not be believed. But at least you will be on your guard. My words will sink in, and each fresh event that comes along will confirm your wavering faith. It was necessary for me to speak now—later I might not have been able to do so."

"You mean—?" asked Crowther, impressed in spite of himself by the gravity of Poirot's tone.

"I mean, monsieur, that since I have penetrated the identity of Number Four, my life is not worth an hour's purchase. He will seek to destroy me at all costs—and not for nothing is he named 'The Destroyer.' Messieurs, I salute you. To you, M. Crowther, I deliver this key, and this sealed envelope. I have got together all my notes on the case, and my ideas as to how best to meet the menace that any day may break upon the world, and have placed them in a certain safe deposit. In the event of my death, M. Crowther, I authorise you to take charge of those papers and make what use you can of them. And now, messieurs, I wish you good day."

Desjardeaux merely bowed coldly, but Crowther sprang up and held out his hand.

"You have converted me, M. Poirot. Fantastic as the whole thing seems, I believe utterly in the truth of what you have told us."

Ingles left at the same time as we did.

"I am not disappointed with the interview," said Poirot, as we walked along. "I did not expect to convince Desjardeaux, but I have at least ensured that, if I die, my knowledge does not die with me. And I have made one or two converts. *Pas si mal!"*

"I'm with you, as you know," said Ingles. "By the way, I'm going out to China as soon as I can get off."

"Is that wise?"

"No," said Ingles dryly. "But it's necessary. One must do what one can."

"Ah, you are a brave man!" cried Poirot with emotion. "If we were not in the street, I would embrace you."

I fancied that Ingles looked rather relieved.

"I don't suppose that I shall be in any more danger in China than you are in London," he growled.

"That is possibly true enough," admitted Poirot. "I hope that they will not succeed in massacring Hastings also, that is all. That would annoy me greatly."

I interrupted this cheerful conversation to remark that I had no intention of letting myself be massacred, and shortly afterwards Ingles parted from us.

For some time we went along in silence, which Poirot at length broke by uttering a totally unexpected remark.

"I think—I really think—that I shall have to bring my brother into this."

"Your brother," I cried, astonished. "I never knew you had a brother?"

"You surprise me, Hastings. Do you not know that all celebrated detectives have brothers who would be even more celebrated than they are were it not for constitutional indolence?"

Poirot employs a peculiar manner sometimes which makes it well-nigh impossible to know whether he is jesting or in earnest. That manner was very evident at the moment.

"What is your brother's name?" I asked, trying to adjust myself to this new idea.

"Achille Poirot," replied Poirot gravely. "He lives near Spa in Belgium."

"What does he do?" I asked with some curiosity, putting aside a half-formed wonder as to the character and disposition of the late Madame Poirot, and her classical taste in Christian names.

"He does nothing. He is, as I tell, of a singularly indolent disposition. But his abilities are hardly less than my own—which is saying a great deal."

"Is he like you to look at?"

"Not unlike. But not nearly so handsome. And he wears no moustaches."

"Is he older than you, or younger?"

"He happens to have been born on the same day."

"A twin," I cried.

"Exactly, Hastings. You jump to the right conclusion with unfailing accuracy. But here we are at home again. Let us at once get to work on that little affair of the Duchess's necklace."

But the Duchess's necklace was doomed to wait awhile. A case of quite another description was waiting for us.

Our landlady, Mrs. Pearson, at once informed us that a hospital nurse had called and was waiting to see Poirot.

We found her sitting in the big arm-chair facing the window, a pleasant-faced woman of middle age in a dark blue uniform. She was a little reluctant to come to the point, but Poirot soon put her at her ease, and she embarked upon her story.

"You see, M. Poirot, I've never come across anything of the kind before. I was sent for, from the Lark Sisterhood, to go down to a case in Hertfordshire. An old gentleman it is, Mr. Templeton. Quite a pleasant house, and quite pleasant people. The wife, Mrs. Templeton, is much younger than her husband, and he has a son by his first marriage who lives there. I don't know that the young man and the step-mother always get on together. He's not quite what you'd call normal—not 'wanting' exactly, but decidedly dull in the intellect. Well, this illness of Mr. Templeton's seemed to me from the first to be very mysterious. At times there seemed really nothing the matter with him, and then he suddenly has one of these gastric attacks with pain and vomiting. But the doctor seemed quite satisfied, and it wasn't for me to say anything. But I couldn't help thinking about it. And then—"

She paused, and became rather red.

"Something happened which aroused your suspicions?" suggested Poirot.

"Yes."

But she still seemed to find it difficult to go on.

"I found the servants were passing remarks too."

"About Mr. Templeton's illness?"

"Oh, no! About—about this other thing—"

"Mrs. Templeton?"

"Yes."

"Mrs. Templeton and the doctor, perhaps?"

Poirot had an uncanny flair in these things. The nurse threw him a grateful glance and went on.

"They *were* passing remarks. And then one day I happened to see them together myself—in the garden—"

It was left at that. Our client was in such an agony of outraged propriety that no one could feel it necessary to ask exactly what she had seen in the garden. She had evidently seen quite enough to make up her own mind on the situation.

"The attacks got worse and worse. Dr. Treves said it was all perfectly natural and to be expected, and that Mr. Templeton could not possibly live long, but I've never seen anything like it before myself—not in all my long experience of nursing. It seemed to me much more like some form of—"

She paused, hesitating.

"Arsenical poisoning?" said Poirot helpfully.

She nodded.

"And then, too, he, the patient, I mean, said something queer. 'They'll do for me, the four of them. They'll do for me yet.' "

"Eh?" said Poirot quickly.

"Those were his very words, M. Poirot. He was in

great pain at the time, of course, and hardly knew what he was saying."

" 'They'll do for me, the four of them,' " repeated Poirot thoughtfully. "What did he mean by 'the four of them,' do you think?"

"That I can't say, M. Poirot. I thought perhaps he meant his wife and son, and the doctor, and perhaps Miss Clark, Mrs. Templeton's companion. That would make four, wouldn't it? He might think they were all in league against him."

"Quite so, quite so," said Poirot, in a preoccupied voice. "What about food? Could you take no precautions about that?"

"I'm always doing what I can. But, of course, sometimes Mrs. Templeton insists on bringing him his food herself, and then there are the times when I am off duty."

"Exactly. And you are not sure enough of your ground to go to the police?"

The nurse's face showed her horror at the mere idea.

"What I have done, M. Poirot, is this. Mr. Templeton had a very bad attack after partaking of a bowl of soup. I took a little from the bottom of the bowl afterwards, and have brought it up with me. I have been spared for the day to visit a sick mother, as Mr. Templeton was well enough to be left."

She drew out a little bottle of dark fluid and handed it to Poirot.

"Excellent, mademoiselle. We will have this analysed immediately. If you will return here in, say, an hour's time I think that we shall be able to dispose of your suspicions one way or another."

First extracting from our visitor her name and qualifications, he ushered her out. Then he wrote a note and sent it off together with the bottle of soup. Whilst we waited to hear the result, Poirot amused himself by verifying the nurse's credentials, somewhat to my surprise.

"No, no, my friend," he declared. "I do well to be careful. Do not forget the Big Four are on our track."

However, he soon elicited the information that a nurse of the name of Mabel Palmer was a member of the Lark Institute and had been sent to the case in question.

"So far, so good," he said, with a twinkle. "And now here comes Nurse Palmer back again, and here also is our analyst's report."

Both the nurse and I waited anxiously whilst Poirot read the analyst's report.

"Is there arsenic in it?" she asked breathlessly.

Poirot shook his head, refolding the paper.

"No."

We were both immeasurably surprised.

"There is no arsenic in it," continued Poirot. "But there is antimony. And that being the case, we will start immediately for Hertfordshire. Pray Heaven that we are not too late."

It was decided that the simplest plan was for Poirot to represent himself truly as a detective, but that the ostensible reason of his visit should be to question Mrs. Templeton about a servant formerly in her employment whose name he obtained from Nurse Palmer, and who he could represent as being concerned in a jewel robbery.

It was late when we arrived at Elmstead, as the house was called. We had allowed Nurse Palmer to precede us by about twenty minutes, so that there should be no question of our all arriving together.

Mrs. Templeton, a tall dark woman, with sinuous movements and uneasy eyes, received us. I noticed that as Poirot announced his profession, she drew in her breath with a sudden hiss, as though badly startled, but she answered his question about the maid-servant readily enough. And then, to test her, Poirot embarked upon a long history of a poisoning case in which a guilty wife had figured. His eyes never left her face as he talked, and try as she would, she could hardly conceal her rising agitation. Suddenly, with an incoherent word of excuse, she hurried from the room.

We were not long left alone. A squarely-built man with a small red moustache and pince-nez came in.

"Dr. Treves," he introduced himself. "Mrs. Templeton asked me to make her excuses to you. She's in a very bad state, you know. Nervous strain. Worry over her husband and all that. I've prescribed bed and bromide. But she hopes you'll stay and take pot luck, and I'm to do host. We've heard of you down here, M. Poirot, and we mean to make the most of you. Ah, here's Micky!"

A shambling young man entered the room. He had a very round face, and foolish-looking eyebrows raised as though in perpetual surprise. He grinned awkwardly as he shook hands. This was clearly the "wanting" son.

Presently we all went in to dinner. Dr. Treves left the room—to open some wine, I think—and suddenly the boy's physiognomy underwent a startling change. He leant forward, staring at Poirot.

"You've come about father," he said, nodding his head. "*I* know. I know lots of things—but nobody thinks I do. Mother will be glad when father's dead and she can marry Dr. Treves. She isn't my own mother, you know. I don't like her. She wants father to die."

It was all rather horrible. Luckily, before Poirot had time to reply, the doctor came back, and we had to carry on a forced conversation.

And then suddenly Poirot lay back in his chair with a hollow groan. His face was contorted with pain.

"My dear sir, what's the matter?" cried the doctor.

"A sudden spasm. I am used to them. No, no, I require no assistance from you, doctor. If I might lie down upstairs."

His request was instantly acceded to, and I accompanied him upstairs, where he collapsed on the bed, groaning heavily.

For the first minute or two I had been taken in, but I had quickly realised that Poirot was—as he would have put it—playing the comedy, and that his object was to be left alone upstairs near the patient's room.

Hence I was quite prepared when, the instant we were alone, he sprang up.

"Quick, Hastings, the window. There is ivy outside. We can climb down before they begin to suspect."

"Climb down?"

"Yes, we must get out of this house at once. You saw him at dinner?"

"The doctor?"

"No, young Templeton. His trick with his bread. Do you remember what Flossie Monro told us before she died? That Claud Darrell had a habit of dabbing his bread on the table to pick up crumbs. Hastings, this is a vast plot, and that vacant-looking young man is our arch enemy—Number Four! Hurry."

I did not wait to argue. Incredible as the whole thing seemed, it was wiser not to delay. We scrambled down the ivy as quietly as we could and made a bee-line for the small town and the railway station. We were just able to catch the last train, the 8:34 which would land us in town about eleven o'clock.

"A plot," said Poirot thoughtfully. "How many of them were in it, I wonder? I suspect that the whole Templeton family are just so many agents of the Big Four. Did they simply want to decoy us down there? Or was it more subtle than that? Did they intend to play the comedy down there and keep me interested until they had had time to do—what? I wonder now."

He remained very thoughtful.

Arrived at our lodgings, he restrained me at the door of the sitting-room.

"Attention, Hastings. I have my suspicions. Let me enter first."

He did so, and, to my slight amusement, took the precaution to press on the electric switch with an old galosh. Then he went round the room like a strange cat, cautiously, delicately, on the alert for danger. I watched him for some time, remaining obediently where I had been put by the wall.

"It's all right, Poirot," I said impatiently.

"It seems so, *mon ami*, it seems so. But let us make sure."

"Rot," I said. "I shall light the fire, anyway, and have a pipe. I've caught you out for once. You had the matches last and you didn't put them back in the holder as usual—the very thing you're always cursing me for doing."

I stretched out my hand. I heard Poirot's warning cry—saw him leaping towards me—my hand touched the match-box.

Then—a flash of blue flame—an ear-rending crash—and darkness—

I came to myself to find the familiar face of our old friend Dr. Ridgeway bending over me. An expression of relief passed over his features.

"Keep still," he said soothingly. "You're all right. There's been an accident, you know."

"Poirot?" I murmured.

"You're in my digs. Everything's quite all right."

A cold fear clutched at my heart. His evasion woke a horrible fear.

"Poirot?" I reiterated. "What of Poirot?"

He saw that I had to know and that further evasions were useless.

"By a miracle you escaped—Poirot—did not!"

A cry burst from my lips.

"Not dead? Not dead?"

Ridgeway bowed his head, his features working with emotion.

With desperate energy I pulled myself to a sitting position.

"Poirot may be dead," I said weakly. "But his spirit lives on. I will carry on his work! Death to the Big Four!"

Then I fell back, fainting.

Chapter XVI

The Dying Chinaman

EVEN now I can hardly bear to write of those days in March.

Poirot—the unique, the inimitable Hercule Poirot—dead! There was a particularly diabolical touch in the disarranged match-box, which was certain to catch his eye, and which he would hasten to rearrange—and thereby touch off the explosion. That, as a matter of fact, it was I who actually precipitated the catastrophe never ceased to fill me with unavailing remorse. It was, as Doctor Ridgeway said, a perfect miracle that I had not been killed, but had escaped with a slight concussion.

Although it had seemed to me as though I regained consciousness almost immediately, it was in reality over twenty-four hours before I came back to life. It was not until the evening of the day following that I was able to stagger feebly into an adjoining room, and view with deep emotion the plain elm coffin which held the remains of one of the most marvellous men this world has ever known.

From the very first moment of regaining consciousness I had only one purpose in mind—to avenge Poirot's death, and to hunt down the Big Four remorselessly.

I had thought that Ridgeway would have been of one mind with me about this, but to my surprise the good doctor seemed unaccountably lukewarm.

"Get back to South America" was his advice, tendered

152

on every occasion. Why attempt the impossible? Put as delicately as possible, his opinion amounted to this:—If Poirot, the unique Poirot, had failed, was it likely that I should succeed?

But I was obstinate. Putting aside any question as to whether I had the necessary qualifications for the task (and I may say in passing that I did not entirely agree with his views on this point), I had worked so long with Poirot that I knew his methods by heart, and felt fully capable of taking up the work where he had laid it down; it was, with me, a question of feeling. My friend had been foully murdered. Was I to go tamely back to South America without an effort to bring his murderers to justice?

I said all this and more to Ridgeway, who listened attentively enough.

"All the same," he said when I had finished, "my advice does not vary. I am earnestly convinced that Poirot himself, if he were here, would urge you to return. In his name, I beg of you, Hastings, abandon these wild ideas and go back to your ranch."

To that only one answer was possible, and, shaking his head sadly, he said no more.

It was a month before I was fully restored to health. Towards the end of April, I sought, and obtained, an interview with the Home Secretary.

Mr. Crowther's manner was reminiscent of that of Dr. Ridgeway. It was soothing and negative. Whilst appreciating the offer of my services, he gently and considerately declined them. The papers referred to by Poirot had passed into his keeping, and he assured me that all possible steps were being taken to deal with the approaching menace.

With that cold comfort I was forced to be satisfied. Mr. Crowther ended the interview by urging me to return to South America. I found the whole thing profoundly unsatisfactory.

I should, I suppose, in its proper place, have described Poirot's funeral. It was a solemn and moving ceremony, and the extraordinary number of floral tributes passed belief. They came from high and low alike, and bore striking testimony to the place my friend had made for himself in the country of his adoption. For myself, I was frankly overcome by emotion as I stood by the grave side and thought of all our varied experiences and the happy days we had passed together.

By the beginning of May I had mapped out a plan of campaign. I felt that I could not do better than keep Poirot's scheme of advertising for any information respecting Claud Darrell. I had an advertisement to this effect inserted in a number of morning newspapers, and I was sitting in a small restaurant in Soho, and judging of the effect of the advertisement, when a small paragraph in another part of the paper gave me a nasty shock.

Very briefly, it reported the mysterious disappearance of Mr. John Ingles from the S.S. *Shanghai,* shortly after the latter had left Marseilles. Although the weather was perfectly smooth, it was feared that the unfortunate gentleman must have fallen overboard. The paragraph ended with a brief reference to Mr. Ingles's long and distinguished service in China.

The news was unpleasant. I read into Ingles's death a sinister motive. Not for one moment did I believe the theory of an accident. Ingles had been murdered, and his death was only too clearly the handiwork of that accursed Big Four.

As I sat there, stunned by the blow, and turning the whole matter over in my mind, I was startled by the remarkable behaviour of the man sitting opposite me. So far I had not paid much attention to him. He was a thin, dark man of middle age, sallow of complexion, with a small pointed beard. He had sat down opposite me so quietly that I had hardly noticed his arrival.

But his actions now were decidedly peculiar, to say the least of them. Leaning forward, he deliberately helped me to salt, putting it in four little heaps round the edge of my plate.

"You will excuse me," he said, in a melancholy voice. "To help a stranger to salt is to help them to sorrow, they say. That may be an unavoidable necessity. I hope not, though. I hope that you will be reasonable."

Then, with a certain significance, he repeated his operations with the salt on his own plate. The symbol 4 was too plain to be missed. I looked at him searchingly. In no way that I could see did he resemble young Templeton, or James the footman, or any other of the various personalities we had come across. Nevertheless, I was convinced that I had to do with no less than the redoubtable Number Four himself. In his voice there was certainly a faint resemblance to the buttoned-up stranger who had called upon us in Paris.

I looked round, undecided as to my course of action. Reading my thoughts, he smiled and gently shook his head.

"I should not advise it," he remarked. "Remember what came of your hasty action in Paris. Let me assure you that my way of retreat is well assured. Your ideas are inclined to be a little crude, Captain Hastings, if I may say so."

"You devil," I said, choking with rage, "you incarnate devil!"

"Heated—just a trifle heated. Your late lamented friend would have told you that a man who keeps calm has always a great advantage."

"You dare to speak of him," I cried. "The man you murdered so foully. And you come here—"

He interrupted me.

"I came here for an excellent and peaceful purpose. To advise you to return at once to South America. If you do so, that is the end of the matter as far as the Big Four are concerned. You and yours will not be molested in any way. I give you my word as to that."

I laughed scornfully.

"And if I refuse to obey your autocratic command?"

"It is hardly a command. Shall we say that it is—a warning?"

There was a cold menace in his tone.

"The first warning," he said softly. "You will be well advised not to disregard it."

Then, before I had any hint of his intention, he rose and slipped quickly away towards the door. I sprang to my feet and was after him in a second but by bad luck I cannoned straight into an enormously fat man who blocked the way between me and the next table. By the time I had disentangled myself, my quarry was just passing through the doorway, and the next delay was from a waiter carrying a huge pile of plates who crashed into me without the least warning. By the time I got to the door there was no sign of the thin man with the dark beard.

The waiter was fulsome in apologies, the fat man was sitting placidly at a table ordering his lunch. There was nothing to show that both occurrences had not been a pure accident. Nevertheless, I had my own opinion as to that. I knew well enough that the agents of the Big Four were everywhere.

Needless to say, I paid no heed to the warning given me. I would do or die in the good cause. I received in all only two answers to the advertisements. Neither of them gave me any information of value. They were both from actors who had played with Claud Darrell at one time or another. Neither of them knew him at all intimately, and no new light was thrown upon the problem of his identity and present whereabouts.

No further sign came from the Big Four until about ten days later. I was crossing Hyde Park, lost in thought, when a voice, rich with a persuasive foreign inflection, hailed me.

"Captain Hastings, is it not?"

A big limousine had just drawn up by the pavement. A woman was leaning out. Exquisitely dressed in black, with

wonderful pearls, I recognised the lady first known to us as
Countess Vera Rossakoff, and afterwards under a different
alias as an agent of the Big Four. Poirot, for some reason or
other, had always had a sneaking fondness for the countess. Something in her very flamboyance attracted the little
man. She was, he was wont to declare in moments of
enthusiasm, a woman in a thousand. That she was arrayed
against us, on the side of our bitterest enemies, never
seemed to weigh in his judgment. "Ah, do not pass on!"
said the countess. "I have something most important to say
to you. And do not try to have me arrested either, for that
would be stupid. You were always a little stupid—yes, yes,
it is so. You are stupid now, when you persist in disregard-
ing the warning we sent you. It is the second warning I
bring you. Leave England at once. You can do no good
here—I tell you that frankly. You will never accomplish
anything."

"In that case," I said stiffly, "it seems rather extraordinary that you are all so anxious to get me out of the
country."

The countess shrugged her shoulders—magnificent
shoulders, and a magnificent gesture.

"For my part, I think that, too, stupid. I would leave
you here to play about happily. But the chiefs, you see, are
fearful that some word of yours may give great help to
those more intelligent than yourself. Hence—you are to be
banished."

The countess appeared to have a flattering idea of my
abilities. I concealed my annoyance. Doubtless this attitude
of hers was assumed expressly to annoy me and to give me
the idea that I was unimportant.

"It would, of course, be quite easy to—remove you,"
she continued, "but I am quite sentimental sometimes. I
pleaded for you. You have a nice little wife somewhere,
have you not? And it would please the poor little man who
is dead to know that you were not to be killed. I always
liked him, you know. He was clever—but clever! Had it not

been a case of four against one I honestly believe he might have been too much for us. I confess it frankly—he was my master! I sent a wreath to the funeral as a token of my admiration—an enormous one of crimson roses. Crimson roses express my temperament."

I listened in silence and a growing distaste.

"You have the look of a mule when it puts its ears back and kicks. Well, I have delivered my warning. Remember this, the third warning will come by the hand of the Destroyer—"

She made a sign, and the car whirled away rapidly. I noted the number mechanically, but without the hope that it would lead to anything. The Big Four were not apt to be careless in details.

I went home a little sobered. One fact had emerged from the countess's flood of volubility. I was in real danger of my life. Though I had no intention of abandoning the struggle, I saw that it behoved me to walk warily and adopt every possible precaution.

Whilst I was reviewing all these facts and seeking for the best line of action, the telephone bell rang. I crossed the room and picked up the receiver.

"Yes. Hallo. Who's speaking?"

A crisp voice answered me.

"This is St. Giles' Hospital. We have a Chinaman here, knifed in the street and brought in. He can't last long. We rang you up because we found in his pocket a piece of paper with your name and address on it."

I was very much astonished. Nevertheless, after a moment's reflection I said that I would come down at once. St. Giles' Hospital was, I knew, down by the docks, and it occurred to me that the Chinaman might have just come off some ship.

It was on my way down there that a sudden suspicion shot into my mind. Was the whole thing a trap? Wherever a Chinaman was, there might be the hand of Li Chang Yen.

I remembered the adventure of the Baited Trap. Was the whole thing a ruse on the part of my enemies?

A little reflection convinced me that at any rate a visit to the hospital would do no harm. It was probable that the thing was not so much a plot as what is vulgarly known as a "plant." The dying Chinaman would make some revelation to me upon which I should act, and which would have the result of leading me into the hands of the Big Four. The thing to do was to preserve an open mind, and whilst feigning credulity be secretly on my guard.

On arriving at St. Giles' Hospital, and making my business known, I was taken at once to the accident ward, to the bedside of the man in question. He lay absolutely still, his eyelids closed, and only a very faint movement of the chest showed that he still breathed. A doctor stood by the bed, his fingers on the Chinaman's pulse.

"He's almost gone," he whispered to me. "You know him, eh?"

I shook my head.

"I've never seen him before."

"Then what was he doing with your name and address in his pocket? You are Captain Hastings, aren't you?"

"Yes, but I can't explain it any more than you can."

"Curious thing. From his papers he seems to have been the servant of a man called Ingles—a retired Civil Servant. Ah, you know him, do you?" he added quickly, as I started at the name.

Ingles's servant! Then I *had* seen him before. Not that I had ever succeeded in being able to distinguish one Chinaman from another. He must have been with Ingles on his way to China, and after the catastrophe he had returned to England with a message, possibly, for me. It was vital, imperative that I should hear that message.

"Is he conscious?" I asked. "Can he speak? Mr. Ingles was an old friend of mine, and I think it possible that this poor fellow has brought me a message from him. Mr. Ingles is believed to have gone overboard about ten days ago."

"He's just conscious, but I doubt if he has the force to speak. He lost a terrible lot of blood, you know. I can administer a stimulant, of course, but we've already done all that is possible in that direction."

Nevertheless, he administered a hypodermic injection, and I stayed by the bed, hoping against hope for a word—a sign—that might be of the utmost value to me in my work. But the minutes sped on and no sign came.

And suddenly a baleful idea shot across my mind. Was I not already falling into the trap? Suppose that this Chinaman had merely assumed the part of Ingles's servant, that he was in reality an agent of the Big Four? Had I not once read that certain Chinese priests were capable of simulating death? Or, to go further still, Li Chang Yen might command a little band of fanatics who would welcome death itself if it came at the command of their master. I must be on my guard.

Even as these thoughts flashed across my mind, the man in the bed stirred. His eyes opened. He murmured something incoherently. Then I saw his glance fasten upon me. He made no sign of recognition, but I was at once aware that he was trying to speak to me. Be he friend or foe, I must hear what he had to say.

I leaned over the bed, but the broken sounds conveyed no sort of meaning to me. I thought I caught the word "hand," but in what connection it was used I could not tell. Then it came again, and this time I heard another word, the word "Largo." I stared in amazement, as the possible juxtaposition of the two suggested itself to me.

"Handel's Largo?" I queried.

The Chinaman's eyelids flickered rapidly, as though in assent, and he added another Italian word, the word "carrozza." Two or three more words of murmured Italian came to my ears, and then he fell back abruptly.

The doctor pushed me aside. It was all over. The man was dead.

I went out into the air again thoroughly bewildered.

"Handel's Largo," and a "*carrozza.*" If I remembered rightly, a *carrozza* was a carriage. What possible meaning could lie behind those simple words. The man was a Chinaman, not an Italian, why should he speak in Italian? Surely, if he were indeed Ingles's servant, he must know English? The whole thing was profoundly mystifying. I puzzled over it all the way home. Oh, if only Poirot had been there to solve the problem with his lightning ingenuity!

I let myself in with my latch-key and went slowly up to my room. A letter was lying on the table, and I tore it open carelessly enough. But in a minute I stood rooted to the ground whilst I read.

It was a communication from a firm of solicitors.

"DEAR SIR (it ran),—As instructed by our late client, M. Hercule Poirot, we forward you the enclosed letter. This letter was placed in our hands a week before his death, with instructions that in the event of his demise, it should be sent to you at a certain date after his death.
"Yours faithfully, etc."

I turned the enclosed missive over and over. It was undoubtedly from Poirot. I knew that familiar writing only too well. With a heavy heart, yet a certain eagerness, I tore it open.

"MON CHER AMI (it began),—When you receive this I shall be no more. Do not shed tears about me, but follow my orders. Immediately upon receipt of this, return to South America. Do not be pig-headed about this. It is not for sentimental reasons that I bid you undertake the journey. *It is necessary.* It is part of the plan of Hercule Poirot! To say more is unnecessary, to any one who has the acute intelligence of my friend Hastings.

"*A bas* the Big Four! I salute you, my friend, from beyond the grave.

"Ever thine,

"HERCULE POIROT."

I read and re-read this astonishing communication. One thing was evident. This amazing man had so provided for every eventuality that even his own death did not upset the sequence of his plans! Mine was to be the active part—his the directing genius. Doubtless I should find full instructions awaiting me beyond the seas. In the meantime my enemies, convinced that I was obeying their warning, would cease to trouble their heads about me. I could return, unsuspected, and work havoc in their midst.

There was now nothing to hinder my immediate departure. I sent off cables, booked my passage, and one week later found me embarking in the *Ansonia* en route for Buenos Ayres.

Just as the boat left the quay, a steward brought me a note. It had been given him, so he explained, by a big gentleman in a fur coat who had left the boat last thing before the gangway planks were lifted.

I opened it. It was terse and to the point.

"You are wise," it ran. It was signed with a big figure 4.

I could afford to smile to myself!

The sea was not too choppy. I enjoyed a passable dinner, made up my mind as to the majority of my fellow passengers, and had a rubber or two of Bridge. Then I turned in and slept like a log as I always do on board ship.

I was awakened by feeling myself persistently shaken. Dazed and bewildered, I saw that one of the ship's officers was standing over me. He gave a sigh of relief as I sat up.

"Thank the Lord I've got you awake at last. I've had no end of a job. Do you always sleep like that?"

"What's the matter?" I asked, still bewildered and not fully awake. "Is there anything wrong with the ship?"

"I expect you know what's the matter better than I do," he replied dryly. "Special instructions from the Admiralty. There's a destroyer waiting to take you off."

"What?" I cried. "In mid-ocean?"

"It seems a most mysterious affair, but that's not my business. They've sent a young fellow aboard who is to take your place, and we are all sworn to secrecy. Will you get up and dress?"

Utterly unable to conceal my amazement I did as I was told. A boat was lowered, and I was conveyed aboard the destroyer. There I was received courteously, but got no further information. The commander's instructions were to land me at a certain spot on the Belgian coast. There his knowledge and responsibility ended.

The whole thing was like a dream. The one idea I held to firmly was that all this must be part of Poirot's plan. I must simply go forward blindly, trusting in my dead friend.

I was duly landed at the spot indicated. There a motor was waiting, and soon I was rapidly whirling along across the flat Flemish plains. I slept that night at a small hotel in Brussels. The next day we went on again. The country became wooded and hilly. I realised that we were penetrating into the Ardennes, and I suddenly remembered Poirot's saying that he had a brother who lived at Spa.

But we did not go to Spa itself. We left the main road and wound into the leafy fastnesses of the hills, till we reached a little hamlet, and an isolated white villa high on the hill-side. Here the car stopped in front of the green door of the villa.

The door opened as I alighted. An elderly man-servant stood in the doorway bowing.

"M. le Capitaine Hastings?" he said in French. "Monsieur le Capitaine is expected. If he will follow me."

He led the way across the hall, and flung open a door at the back, standing aside to let me pass in.

I blinked a little, for the room faced west and the afternoon sun was pouring in. Then my vision cleared and

I saw a figure waiting to welcome me with outstretched hands.

It was—oh, impossible, it couldn't be—but yes!

"Poirot!" I cried, and for once did not attempt to evade the embrace with which he overwhelmed me.

"But yes, but yes, it is indeed I! Not so easy to kill Hercule Poirot!"

"But Poirot—*why*?"

"A *ruse de guerre*, my friend, a *ruse de guerre*. All is now ready for our grand coup."

"But you might have told *me*!"

"No, Hastings, I could not. Never, never, in a thousand years, could you have acted the part at the funeral. As it was, it was perfect. It could not fail to carry conviction to the Big Four."

"But what I've been through—"

"Do not think me too unfeeling. I carried out the deception partly for your sake. I was willing to risk my own life, but I had qualms about continually risking yours. So, after the explosion, I have an idea of great brilliancy. The good Ridgeway, he enables me to carry it out. I am dead, you will return to South America. But, *mon ami*, that is just what you would not do. In the end I have to arrange a solicitor's letter, and a long rigmarole. But, at all events, here you are—that is the great thing. And now we lie here—*perdu*—till the moment comes for the last grand coup—the final overthrowing of the Big Four."

Chapter XVII

Number Four
Wins a Trick

FROM our quiet retreat in the Ardennes we watched the progress of affairs in the great world. We were plentifully supplied with newspapers, and every day Poirot received a bulky envelope, evidently containing some kind of report. He never showed these reports to me, but I could usually tell from his manner whether its contents had been satisfactory or otherwise. He never wavered in his belief that our present plan was the only one likely to be crowned by success.

"As a minor point, Hastings," he remarked one day, "I was in continual fear of your death lying at my door. And that rendered me nervous—like a cat upon the jumps, as you say. But now I am well satisfied. Even if they discover that the Captain Hastings who landed in South America is an imposter (and I do not think they will discover it, they are not likely to send an agent out there who knows you personally), they will only believe that you are trying to circumvent them in some clever manner of your own, and will pay no serious attention to discovering your whereabouts. Of the one vital fact, my supposed death, they are thoroughly convinced. They will go ahead and mature their plans."

"And then?" I asked eagerly.

"And then, *mon ami*, grand resurrection of Hercule Poirot! At the eleventh hour I reappear, throw all into confusion, and achieve the supreme victory in my own unique manner!"

I realised that Poirot's vanity was of the case-hardened variety which could withstand all attacks. I reminded him that once or twice the honours of the game had lain with our adversaries. But I might have known that it was impossible to diminish Hercule Poirot's enthusiasm for his own methods.

"See you, Hastings, it is like the little trick that you play with the cards. You have seen it without doubt? You take the four knaves, you divide them, one on top of the pack, one underneath, and so on—you cut and you shuffle, and there they are all together again. That is my object. So far I have been contending, now against one of the Big Four, now against another. But let me get them all together, like the four knaves in the pack of cards, and then, with one coup, I destroy them all!"

"And how do you propose to get them all together?" I asked.

"By awaiting the supreme moment. By lying *perdu* until they are ready to strike."

"That may mean a long wait," I grumbled.

"Always impatient, the good Hastings! But no, it will not be so long. The one man they were afraid of—myself—is out of the way. I give them two or three months at most."

His speaking of some one being got out of the way reminded me of Ingles and his tragic death, and I remembered that I had never told Poirot about the dying Chinaman in St. Giles' Hospital.

He listened with keen attention to my story.

"Ingles's servant, eh? And the few words he uttered were in Italian? Curious."

"That's why I suspected it might have been a plant on the part of the Big Four."

"Your reasoning is at fault, Hastings. Employ the little gray cells. If your enemies wished to deceive you they would assuredly have seen to it that the Chinaman spoke in intelligible pigeon English. No, the message was genuine. Tell me again all that you heard?"

"First of all he made a reference to Handel's Largo, and then he said something that sounded like '*carrozza*'— that's a carriage, isn't it?"

"Nothing else?"

"Well, just at the end he murmured something like 'Cara' somebody or other—some woman's name. Zia, I think. But I don't suppose that that had any bearing on the rest of it."

"You would not suppose so, Hastings. Cara Zia is very important, very important indeed."

"I don't see—"

"My dear friend, you *never* see—and anyway the English know no geography."

"Geography?" I cried. "What has geography got to do with it?"

"I dare say M. Thomas Cook would be more to the point."

As usual, Poirot refused to say anything more—a most irritating trick of his. But I noticed that his manner became extremely cheerful, as though he had scored some point or other.

The days went on, pleasant if a trifle monotonous. There were plenty of books in the villa, and delightful rambles all around, but I chafed sometimes at the forced inactivity of our life, and marvelled at Poirot's state of placid content. Nothing occurred to ruffle our quiet existence, and it was not until the end of June, well within the limit that Poirot had given them, that we had our news of the Big Four.

A car drove up to the villa early one morning, such an unusual event in our peaceful life that I hurried down to satisfy my curiosity. I found Poirot talking to a pleasant-faced young fellow of about my own age.

He introduced me.

"This is Captain Harvey, Hastings, one of the most famous members of your Intelligence Service."

"Not famous at all, I'm afraid," said the young man, laughing pleasantly.

"Not famous except to those in the know, I should have said. Most of Captain Harvey's friends and acquaintances consider him an amiable but brainless young man—devoted only to the trot of the fox or whatever the dance is called."

We both laughed.

"Well, well, to business," said Poirot. "You are of opinion the time has come, then?"

"We are sure of it, sir. China was isolated politically yesterday. What is going on out there, nobody knows. No news of any kind, wireless or otherwise, has come through—just a complete break—and silence!"

"Li Chang Yen has shown his hand. And the others?"

"Abe Ryland arrived in England a week ago, and left for the Continent yesterday."

"And Madame Olivier?"

"Madame Olivier left Paris last night."

"For Italy?"

"For Italy, sir. As far as we can judge, they are both making for the resort you indicated—though how you knew that—"

"Ah, that is not the cap with the feather for me! That was the work of Hastings here. He conceals his intelligence, you comprehend, but it is profound for all that."

Harvey looked at me with due appreciation, and I felt rather uncomfortable.

"All is in train, then," said Poirot. He was pale now, and completely serious. "The time has come. The arrangements are all made?"

"Everything you ordered has been carried out. The governments of Italy, France and England are behind you, and are all working harmoniously together."

"It is, in fact, a new Entente," observed Poirot dryly.

"I am glad that Desjardeaux is convinced at last. *Eh bien,* then, we will start—or rather, I will start. You, Hastings, will remain here—yes, I pray of you. In verity, my friend, I am serious."

I believed him, but it was not likely that I should consent to being left behind in that fashion. Our argument was short but decisive.

It was not until we were in the train, speeding towards Paris that he admitted that he was secretly glad of my decision.

"For you have a part to play, Hastings. An important part! Without you, I might well fail. Nevertheless, I felt that it was my duty to urge you to remain behind."

"There is danger, then?"

"*Mon ami,* where there is the Big Four there is always danger."

On arrival in Paris, we drove across to the Gare de l'Est, and Poirot at last announced our destination. We were bound for Bolzano and Italian Tyrol.

During Harvey's absence from our carriage I took the opportunity of asking Poirot why he had said that the discovery of the rendezvous was my work.

"Because it was, my friend. How Ingles managed to get hold of the information I do not know, but he did, and he sent it to us by his servant. We are bound, *mon ami,* for Karersee, the new Italian name for which is Lago di Carezza. You see now where your 'Cara Zia' comes in and also your 'Carrozza' and 'Largo'—the Handel was supplied by your own imagination. Possibly some reference to the information coming from the 'hand' of M. Ingles started the train of association."

"Karersee?" I queried. "I never heard of it."

"I always tell you that the English know no geography. But as a matter of fact it is a well-known and very beautiful summer resort, four thousand feet up, in the heart of the Dolomites."

"And it is in this out of the way spot that the Big Four have their rendezvous?"

"Say rather their headquarters. The signal has been given, and it is their intention to disappear from the world and issue orders from their mountain fastness. I have made the inquiries—a lot of quarrying of stone and mineral deposits is done there, and the company, apparently a small Italian firm, is in reality controlled by Abe Ryland. I am prepared to swear that a vast subterranean dwelling has been hollowed out in the very heart of the mountain, secret and inaccessible. From there the leaders of the organisation will issue by wireless their orders to their followers who are numbered by the thousands in every country. And from that crag in the Dolomites the dictators of the world will emerge. That is to say—they would emerge were it not for Hercule Poirot."

"Do you seriously believe all this, Poirot? What about the armies and general machinery of civilisation?"

"What about it in Russia, Hastings? This will be Russia on an infinitely larger scale—and with this additional menace—that Madame Olivier's experiments have proceeded further than she has ever given out. I believe that she has, to a certain extent, succeeded in liberating atomic energy and harnessing it to her purpose. Her experiments with the nitrogen of the air have been very remarkable, and she has also experimented in the concentration of wireless energy, so that a beam of great intensity can be focused upon some given spot. Exactly how far she has progressed, nobody knows, but it is certain that it is much farther than has ever been given out. She is a genius, that woman—the Curies were as nothing to her. Add to her genius the powers of Ryland's almost unlimited wealth, and, with the brain of Li Chang Yen, the finest criminal brain ever known, to direct and plan—*eh bien,* it will not be, as you say, all jam for civilisation."

His words made me very thoughtful. Although Poirot was given at times to exaggeration of language, he was not really an alarmist. For the first time I realised what a desperate struggle it was upon which we were engaged.

Harvey soon rejoined us and the journey went on.

We arrived at Bolzano about midday. From there the journey on was by motor. Several big blue motor-cars were waiting in the central square of the town, and we three got into one of them. Poirot, notwithstanding the heat of the day, was muffled to the eyes in greatcoat and scarf. His eyes and the tips of his ears were all that could be seen of him.

I did not know whether this was due to precaution or merely his exaggerated fear of catching a chill. The motor journey took a couple of hours. It was a really wonderful drive. For the first part of the way we wound in and out of huge cliffs, with a trickling waterfall on one hand. Then we emerged into a fertile valley, which continued for some miles, and then, still winding steadily upwards, the bare rocky peaks began to show with dense clustering pine woods at their base. The whole place was wild and lovely. Finally a series of abrupt curves, with the road running through the pine woods on either side, and we came suddenly upon a big hotel and found that we had arrived.

Our rooms had been reserved for us, and under Harvey's guidance we went straight up to them. They looked straight out over the rocky peaks and the long slopes of pine woods leading up to them. Poirot made a gesture towards them.

"It is there?" he asked in a low voice.

"Yes," replied Harvey. "There is a place called the Felsenlabyrynth—all big boulders piled about in a most fantastic way—a path winds through them. The quarrying is to the right of that, but we think that the entrance is probably in the Felsenlabyrynth."

Poirot nodded.

"Come, *mon ami*," he said to me. "Let us go down and sit upon the terrace and enjoy the sunlight."

"You think that wise?" I asked.

He shrugged his shoulders.

The sunlight was marvellous—in fact the glare was almost too great for me. We had some creamy coffee instead of tea, then went upstairs and unpacked our few belongings. Poirot was in his most unapproachable mood, lost in a kind of reverie. Once or twice he shook his head and sighed.

I had been rather intrigued by a man who had got out of our train at Bolzano, and had been met by a private car. He was a small man, and the thing about him that had attracted my attention was that he was almost as much muffled up as Poirot had been. More so, indeed, for in addition to greatcoat and muffler, he was wearing huge blue spectacles. I was convinced that here we had an emissary of the Big Four. Poirot did not seem very impressed by my idea, but when, leaning out of my bedroom window, I reported that the man in question was strolling about in the vicinity of the hotel, he admitted that there might be something in it.

I urged my friend not to go down to dinner, but he insisted on doing so. We entered the dining-room rather late, and were shown to a table by the window. As we sat down, our attention was attracted by an exclamation and a crash of falling china. A dish of *haricots verts* had been upset over a man who was sitting at the table next to ours.

The head waiter came up and was vociferous in apologies.

Presently, when the offending waiter was serving us with soup, Poirot spoke to him.

"An unfortunate accident, that. But it was not your fault."

"Monsieur saw that? No, indeed it was not my fault. The gentleman half sprung up from his chair—I thought he was going to have an attack of some kind. I could not save the catastrophe."

I saw Poirot's eyes shining with the green light I knew so well, and as the waiter departed he said to me in a low voice:—

"You see, Hastings, the effect of Hercule Poirot—alive and in the flesh?"

"You think—"

I had not time to continue. I felt Poirot's hand on my knee, as he whispered excitedly:

"Look, Hastings, look. *His trick with the bread!* Number Four!"

Sure enough, the man at the next table to ours, his face unusually pale, was dabbing a small piece of bread mechanically about the table.

I studied him carefully. His face, clean-shaven and puffily fat, was of a pasty, unhealthy sallowness, with heavy pouches under the eyes and deep lines running from his nose to the corners of his mouth. His age might have been anything from thirty-five to forty-five. In no particular did he resemble any one of the characters which Number Four had previously assumed. Indeed, had it not been for his little trick with the bread, of which he was evidently quite unaware, I would have sworn readily enough that the man sitting there was some one whom I had never seen before.

"He has recognised you," I murmured. "You should not have come down."

"My excellent Hastings, I have feigned death for three months for this one purpose."

"To startle Number Four?"

"To startle him at a moment when he must act quickly or not at all. And we have this great advantage—he does not know that we recognise him. He thinks that he is safe in his new disguise. How I bless Flossie Monro for telling us of that little habit of his."

"What will happen now?" I asked.

"What can happen? He recognises the only man he fears, miraculously resurrected from the dead, at the very minute when the plans of the Big Four are in the balance. Madame Olivier and Abe Ryland lunched here to-day, and it is thought that they went to Cortina. Only we know that they have retired to their hiding place. How much do we know? That is what Number Four is asking himself at this minute. He dare take no risks. I must be suppressed at all costs. *Eh bien,* let him try to suppress Hercule Poirot! I shall be ready for him."

As he finished speaking, the man at the next table got up and went out.

"He has gone to make his little arrangements," said Poirot placidly. "Shall we have our coffee on the terrace, my friend? It would be pleasanter, I think. I will just go up and get a coat."

I went out on to the terrace, a little disturbed in mind. Poirot's assurance did not quite content me. However, so long as we were on our guard, nothing could happen to us. I resolved to keep thoroughly on the alert.

It was quite five minutes before Poirot joined me. With his usual precautions against cold, he was muffled up to the ears. He sat down beside me and sipped his coffee appreciatively.

"Only in England is the coffee so atrocious," he remarked. "On the continent they understand how important it is for the digestion that it should be properly made."

As he finished speaking, the man from the next table suddenly appeared on the terrace. Without any hesitation, he came over and drew up a third chair to our table.

"You do not mind my joining you, I hope," he said in English.

"Not at all, monsieur," said Poirot.

I felt very uneasy. It is true that we were on the terrace of the hotel, with people all round us, but nevertheless I was not satisfied. I sensed the presence of danger.

Meanwhile Number Four chatted away in a perfectly natural manner. It seemed impossible to believe that he was anything but a *bona fide* tourist. He described excursions and motor trips, and posed as quite an authority on the neighbourhood.

He took a pipe from his pocket and began to light it. Poirot drew out his case of tiny cigarettes. As he placed one between his lips, the stranger leant forward with a match.

"Let me give you a light."

As he spoke, without the least warning, all the lights went out. There was a chink of glass, and something pungent under my nose, suffocating me—

CHAPTER XVIII

IN THE
FELSENLABYRYNTH

I could not have been unconscious more than a minute. I came to myself being hustled along between two men. They had me under each arm, supporting my weight, and there was a gag in my mouth. It was pitch dark, but I gathered that we were not outside, but passing through the hotel. All round I could hear people shouting and demanding in every known language what had happened to the lights. My captors swung me down some stairs. We passed along a basement passage, then through a door and out into the open again through a glass door at the back of the hotel. In another moment we had gained the shelter of the pine trees.

I had caught a glimpse of another figure in a similar plight to myself, and realised that Poirot, too, was a victim of this bold coup.

By sheer audacity, Number Four had won the day. He had employed, I gathered, an instant anaesthetic, probably ethyl chloride—breaking a small bulb of it under our noses. Then, in the confusion of the darkness, his accomplices, who had probably been guests sitting at the next table, had thrust gags in our mouths and hurried us away, taking us through the hotel to baffle pursuit.

I cannot describe the hour that followed. We were hurried through the woods at a break-neck pace, going uphill the whole time. At last we emerged in the open, on the mountain-side, and I saw just in front of us an extraordinary conglomeration of fantastic rocks and boulders.

This must be the Felsenlabyrynth of which Harvey had spoken. Soon we were winding in and out of its recesses. The place was like a maze devised by some evil genie.

Suddenly we stopped. An enormous rock barred our path. One of the men stooped and seemed to push on something when, without a sound, the huge mass of rock turned on itself and disclosed a small tunnel-like opening leading into the mountain-side.

Into this we were hurried. For some time the tunnel was narrow, but presently it widened, and before very long we came out into a wide rocky chamber lighted by electricity. There the gags were removed. At a sign from Number Four, who stood facing us with mocking triumph in his face, we were searched and every article was removed from our pockets, including Poirot's little automatic pistol.

A pang smote me as it was tossed down on the table. We were defeated—hopelessly defeated and outnumbered. It was the end.

"Welcome to the headquarters of the Big Four, M. Hercule Poirot," said Number Four in a mocking tone. "To meet you again is an unexpected pleasure. But was it worth while returning from the grave only for this?"

Poirot did not reply. I dared not look at him.

"Come this way," continued Number Four. "Your arrival will be somewhat of a surprise to my colleagues."

He indicated a narrow doorway in the wall. We passed through and found ourselves in another chamber. At the very end of it was a table behind which four chairs were placed. The end chair was empty, but was draped with a mandarin's cape. On the second, smoking a cigar, sat Mr. Abe Ryland. Leaning back in the third chair, with her burning eyes and her nun's face, was Madame Olivier. Number Four took his seat on the fourth chair.

We were in the presence of the Big Four.

Never before had I felt so fully the reality and the presence of Li Chang Yen as I did now when confronting his empty seat. Far away in China, he yet controlled and directed this malign organisation.

Madame Olivier gave a faint cry on seeing us. Ryland, more self-controlled, only shifted his cigar, and raised his grizzled eyebrows.

"M. Hercule Poirot," said Ryland slowly. "This is a pleasant surprise. You put it over on us all right. We thought you were good and buried. No matter, the game is up now."

There was a ring as of steel in his voice. Madame Olivier said nothing, but her eyes burned, and I disliked the slow way she smiled.

"Madame and messieurs, I wish you good-evening," said Poirot quietly.

Something unexpected, something I had not been prepared to hear in his voice made me look at him. He seemed quite composed. Yet there was something about his whole appearance that was different.

Then there was a stir of draperies behind us, and the Countess Vera Rossakoff came in.

"Ah!" said Number Four. "Our valued and trusted lieutenant. An old friend of yours is here, my dear lady."

The countess whirled round with her usual vehemence of movement.

"God in Heaven!" she cried. "It is the little man! Ah! but he has the nine lives of a cat! Oh, little man, little man! Why did you mix yourself up in this?"

"Madame," said Poirot, with a bow. "Me, like the great Napoleon, I am on the side of the big battalions."

As he spoke I saw a sudden suspicion flash into her eyes, and at the same moment I knew the truth which subconsciously I already sensed.

The man beside me was not Hercule Poirot.

He was very like him, extraordinarily like him. There was the same egg-shaped head, the same strutting figure, delicately plump. But the voice was different, and the eyes instead of being green were dark, and surely the moustaches—those famous moustaches—?

My reflections were cut short by the countess's voice. She stepped forward, her voice ringing with excitement.

"You have been deceived. That man is not Hercule Poirot!"

Number Four uttered an incredulous exclamation, but the countess leant forward and snatched at Poirot's moustaches. They came off in her hand, and then, indeed, the truth was plain. For this man's upper lip was disfigured by a small scar which completely altered the expression of the face.

"Not Hercule Poirot," muttered Number Four. "But who can he be then?"

"I know," I cried suddenly, and then stopped dead, afraid I had ruined everything.

But the man I will still refer to as Poirot had turned to me encouragingly.

"Say it if you will. It makes no matter now. The trick has succeeded."

"This is Achille Poirot," I said slowly. "Hercule Poirot's twin brother."

"Impossible," said Ryland sharply, but he was shaken.

"Hercule's plan has succeeded to a marvel," said Achille placidly.

Number Four leapt forward, his voice harsh and menacing.

"Succeeded, has it?" he snarled. "Do you realise that before many minutes have passed you will be dead—dead?"

"Yes," said Achille Poirot gravely. "I realise that. It is you who do not realise that a man may be willing to purchase success by his life. There were men who laid down their lives for their country in the war. I am prepared to lay down mine in the same way for the world."

It struck me just then that although perfectly willing to lay down my life I might have been consulted in the matter. Then I remembered how Poirot had urged me to stay behind, and I felt appeased.

"And in what way will your laying down your life benefit the world?" asked Ryland sardonically.

"I see that you do not perceive the true inwardness of Hercule's plan. To begin with, your place of retreat was known some months ago, and practically all the visitors, hotel assistants and others are detectives or Secret Service men. A cordon has been drawn round the mountain. You may have more than one means of egress, but even so you cannot escape. Poirot himself is directing the operations outside. My boots were smeared with a preparation of aniseed to-night, before I came down to the terrace in my brother's place. Hounds are following the trail. It will lead them infallibly to the rock in the Felsenlabyrynth where the entrance is situated. You see, do what you will to us, the net is drawn tightly round you. You cannot escape."

Madame Olivier laughed suddenly.

"You are wrong. There is one way we can escape, and, like Samson of old, destroy our enemies at the same time. What do you say, my friends?"

Ryland was staring at Achille Poirot.

"Suppose he's lying," he said hoarsely.

The other shrugged his shoulders.

"In an hour it will be dawn. Then you can see for yourself the truth of my words. Already they should have traced me to the entrance in the Felsenlabyrynth."

Even as he spoke, there was a far off reverberation, and a man ran in shouting incoherently. Ryland sprang up and went out. Madame Olivier moved to the end of the room and opened a door that I had not noticed. Inside I caught a glimpse of a perfectly equipped laboratory which reminded me of the one in Paris. Number Four also sprang up and went out. He returned with Poirot's revolver which he gave to the countess.

"There is no danger of their escaping," he said grimly. "But still you had better have this."

Then he went out again.

The countess came over to us and surveyed my companion attentively for some time. Suddenly she laughed.

"You are very clever, M. Achille Poirot," she said mockingly.

"Madame, let us talk business. It is fortunate that they have left us alone together. What is your price?"

"I do not understand. What price?"

"Madame, you can aid us to escape. You know the secret ways out of this retreat. I ask you, what is your price?"

She laughed again.

"More than you could pay, little man! Why, all the money in the world would not buy me!"

"Madame, I did not speak of money. I am a man of intelligence. Nevertheless, this is a true fact—*every one has his price!* In exchange for life and liberty, I offer you your heart's desire."

"So you are a magician!"

"You can call me so if you like."

The countess suddenly dropped her jesting manner. She spoke with passionate bitterness.

"Fool! My heart's desire! Can you give me revenge upon my enemies? Can you give me back youth and beauty and a gay heart? Can you bring the dead to life again?"

Achille Poirot was watching her very curiously.

"Which of the three, Madame? Make your choice."

She laughed sardonically.

"You will sell me the Elixir of Life, perhaps? Come, I will make a bargain with you. Once, I had a child. Find my child for me—and you shall go free."

"Madame, I agree. It is a bargain. Your child shall be restored to you. On the faith of—on the faith of Hercule Poirot himself."

Again that strange woman laughed—this time long and unrestrainedly.

"My dear M. Poirot, I am afraid I laid a little trap for

180

you. It is very kind of you to promise to find my child for me, but, you see, I happen to know that you would not succeed, and so that would be a very one-sided bargain, would it not?"

"Madame, I swear to you by the Holy Angels that I will restore your child to you."

"I asked you before, M. Poirot, could you restore the dead to life?"

"Then the child is—"

"Dead? Yes."

He stepped forward and took her wrist.

"Madame, I—I who speak to you, swear once more. *I will bring the dead to life.*"

She stared at him as though fascinated.

"You do not believe me. I will prove my words. Get my pocket-book which they took from me."

She went out of the room, and returned with it in her hand. Throughout all she retained her grip on the revolver. I felt that Achille Poirot's chances of bluffing her were very slight. The Countess Vera Rossakoff was no fool.

"Open it, madame. The flap on the left-hand side. That is right. Now take out that photograph and look at it."

Wonderingly, she took out what seemed to be a small snapshot. No sooner had she looked at it than she uttered a cry and swayed as though about to fall. Then she almost flew at my companion.

"Where? Where? You shall tell me. Where?"

"Remember your bargain, madame."

"Yes, yes, I will trust you. Quick, before they come back."

Catching him by the hand, she drew him quickly and silently out of the room. I followed. From the outer room she led us into the tunnel by which we had first entered, but a short way along this forked, and she turned off to the right. Again and again the passage divided, but she led us on, never faltering or seeming to doubt her way, and with increasing speed.

"If only we are in time," she panted. "We must be out in the open before the explosion occurs."

Still we went on. I understood that this tunnel led right through the mountain and that we should finally emerge on the other side, facing a different valley. The sweat streamed down my face, but I raced on.

And then, far away, I saw a gleam of daylight. Nearer and nearer. I saw green bushes growing. We forced them aside, pushed our way through. We were in the open again, with the faint light of dawn making everything rosy.

Poirot's cordon was a reality. Even as we emerged, three men fell upon us, but released us again with a cry of astonishment.

"Quick," cried my companion. "Quick—there is no time to lose—"

But he was not destined to finish. The earth shook and trembled under our feet, there was a terrific roar and the whole mountain seemed to dissolve. We were flung headlong through the air.

I came to myself at last. I was in a strange bed and a strange room. Some one was sitting by the window. He turned and came and stood by me.

It was Achille Poirot—or, stay, was it—

The well-known ironical voice dispelled any doubts I might have had.

"But yes, my friend, it is I. Brother Achille has gone home again—to the land of myths. It was I all the time. It is not only Number Four who can act a part. Belladonna in the eyes, the sacrifice of the moustaches, and a real scar the inflicting of which caused me much pain two months ago—but I could not risk a fake beneath the eagle eyes of Number Four. And the final touch, your own knowledge and belief that there was such a person as Achille Poirot! It was invaluable, the assistance you rendered me, half the success of the coup is due to you! The whole crux of the affair was to make them believe that Hercule Poirot was

still at large directing operations. Otherwise, everything
was true, the aniseed, the cordon, etc."

"But why not really send a substitute?"

"And let you go into danger without me by your side?
You have a pretty idea of me there! Besides, I always had a
hope of finding a way out through the countess."

"How on earth did you manage to convince her? It was
a pretty thin story to make her swallow—all that about a
dead child."

"The countess has a great deal more perspicacity than
you have, my dear Hastings. She was taken in at first by
my disguise; but she soon saw through it. When she said,
'You are very clever, M. Achille Poirot,' I knew that she
had guessed the truth. It was then or never to play my
trump card."

"All that rigmarole about bringing the dead to life?"

"Exactly—but then, you see, I had the child all along."

"What?"

"But yes! You know my motto—Be prepared. As soon
as I found that the Countess Rossakoff was mixed up with
the Big Four, I had every possible inquiry made as to her
antecedents. I learnt that she had had a child who was
reported to have been killed, and I also found that there
were discrepancies in the story which led me to wonder
whether it might not, after all, be alive. In the end, I
succeeded in tracing the boy, and by paying out a big sum I
obtained possession of the child's person. The poor little
fellow was nearly dead of starvation. I placed him in a safe
place, with kindly people, and took a snapshot of him in
his new surroundings. And so, when the time came, I had
my little *coup de théâtre* all ready!"

"You are wonderful, Poirot; absolutely wonderful!"

"I was glad to do it, too. For I had admired the countess. I should have been sorry if she had perished in the
explosion."

"I've been half afraid to ask you—what of the Big
Four?"

"All the bodies have now been recovered. That of Number Four was quite unrecognisable, the head blown to pieces. I wish—I rather wish it had not been so. I should have liked to be *sure*—but no more of that. Look at this."

He handed me a newspaper in which a paragraph was marked. It reported the death, by suicide, of Li Chang Yen, who had engineered the recent revolution which had failed so disastrously.

"My great opponent," said Poirot gravely. "It was fated that he and I should never meet in the flesh. When he received the news of the disaster here, he took the simplest way out. A great brain, my friend, a great brain. But I wish I had seen the face of the man who was Number Four. . . . Supposing that, after all—but I romance. He is dead. Yes, *mon ami*, together we have faced and routed the Big Four; and now you will return to your charming wife, and I—I shall retire. The great case of my life is over. Anything else will seem tame after this. No, I shall retire. Possibly I shall grow vegetable marrows! I might even marry and range myself!"

He laughed heartily at the idea, but with a touch of embarrassment. I hope . . . small men always admire big, flamboyant women—

"Marry and range myself," he said again. "Who knows?"

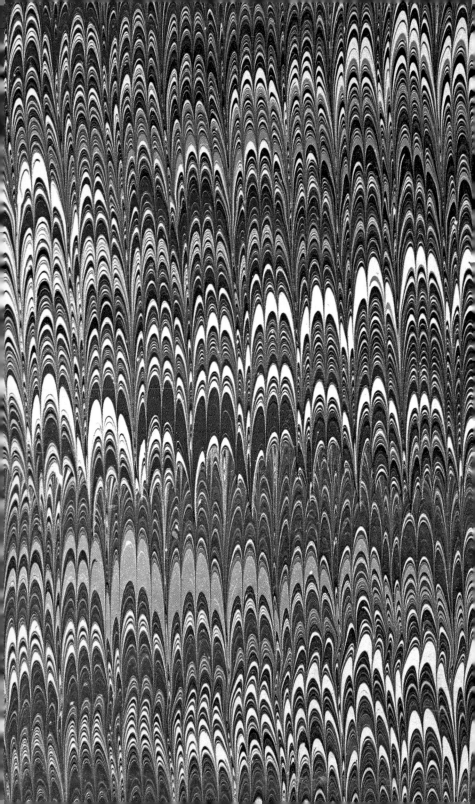